MADE 4 YOU

D0869276

MADE 4 YOU

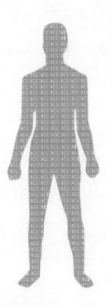

ERIC WALTERS

DCB

Copyright © 2022 Rule of Three Inc.
This edition copyright © 2022 DCB, an imprint of Cormorant Books Inc.

No part of this publication may be reproduced, stored in a retrieval system
or transmitted, in any form or by any means, without the prior written consent
of the publisher or a licence from The Canadian Copyright Licensing
Agency (Access Copyright). For an Access Copyright licence,
visit www.accesscopyright.ca or call toll free 1.800.893.5777.

 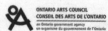

The publisher gratefully acknowledges the support of the Canada Council
for the Arts and the Ontario Arts Council for its publishing program.
We acknowledge the financial support of the Government of Canada
through the Canada Book Fund (CBF) for our publishing activities, and the
Government of Ontario through Ontario Creates, an agency of the Ontario
Ministry of Culture, and the Ontario Book Publishing Tax Credit Program.

LIBRARY AND ARCHIVES CANADA CATALOGUING IN PUBLICATION

Title: Made 4 you / Eric Walters.
Other titles: Made for you
Names: Walters, Eric, 1957– author.
Identifiers: Canadiana (print) 20220190631 | Canadiana (ebook) 20220190666 |
ISBN 9781770866614 (softcover) | ISBN 9781770866621 (HTML)
Classification: LCC PS8595.A598 M36 2022 | DDC jC813/.54—dc23

United States Library of Congress Control Number: 2022934102

Cover design: Angel Guerra / Archetype
Interior text design: Tannice Goddard / tannicegdesigns.ca

Manufactured by Houghton Boston in Saskatoon,
Saskatchewan, Canada in August, 2022.

Printed using paper from a responsible and sustainable resource,
including a mix of virgin fibres and recycled materials.

Printed and bound in Canada.

DCB Young Readers
An imprint of Cormorant Books Inc.
260 SPADINA AVENUE, SUITE 502, TORONTO, ONTARIO, M5T 2E4
www.dcbyoungreaders.com
www.cormorantbooks.com

For my wonderful Anita.
I really was made 4 you.

MADE 4 YOU

1

"DAD, YOU CAN just drop me off here," I said.

"Don't be silly, Becky, your school is just three blocks away."

"You know how busy the drop-off lane can get, and I don't want you to be late for work."

"We're still early, but you have to admit it's a pretty fancy traffic jam with all those BMWs and Porsches. I think our minivan stands out like a sore thumb."

"I like Betsy." That was the name I'd given our van when I was six. I hadn't expected her to stick around this long.

"I was hoping to have traded her in for something newer by now, but, well, you know."

I did know. My father had been laid off from his job the previous year and had only gotten recalled to work a few months ago. Finances had been tight. My parents tried to keep that sort of thing away from me, but I wasn't a kid. I was seventeen.

When my father lost his job, my mother started working more shifts as a personal care worker at the nursing home. Even now she kept up the extra shifts. I thought they were trying to make up for money lost.

"The cars would be different if I was dropping you off at Central," my father said.

Central was the other high school in town. I would have gone there if there hadn't been a boundary change in eighth grade. A couple of streets in our neighborhood got shifted, and suddenly we were going to the same school as the kids from the big houses with rich parents. Most of the friends I'd grown up with and gone to elementary school with went on to Central, and a few of us were shipped to Westfield.

My parents were born and raised in this town and had met when they went to Central. They were high school sweethearts who got married and raised a family. I wasn't going to repeat that pattern unless a boyfriend materialized over the next eight months — not that I was looking for one. I had more important things to take care of during my senior year, especially if I wanted to get a good scholarship.

There was one thing — actually, one person — who'd allowed me to survive the change in high schools: Liv. She was my best friend and one of the few kids who came along with me. We lived two streets apart, and I'd known her since before I even had memories. She'd just always been there.

My father turned in to the sweeping driveway that cut through well-maintained lawns leading to the main entrance. It looked like every Hollywood version of what an upscale high school should look like. There were vehicles, but the traffic hadn't started to back up yet.

"I can't believe parents allow their kids to borrow their expensive cars just to drive to school," my father said.

He didn't seem to know that most of these cars belonged to students.

We came to the drop-off zone. I leaned back and grabbed my backpack. It was heavy with books.

"Thanks, Dad." I undid my seatbelt, gave him a kiss on the cheek, and jumped out.

He started away, leaving behind a slightly blue cloud of exhaust. I looked around to see if anybody had noticed and then instantly felt bad for doing it. I didn't want to care, but still, I did — another reason I was looking forward to getting out of this school, and out of this town.

I walked up the stairs and saw that Liv was sitting by the door, so focused on her phone that she hadn't noticed me. I gave her a little tap with my foot on the sole of her shoe, and she looked up.

"Why are you here so early?" I asked.

"I had to hand in an assignment that was due yesterday."

I looked at my watch. "I have to go to the guidance office. I better get going or I'll be late."

"So what if you're thirty seconds late?" she asked as she got to her feet and fell in beside me as we entered through the main doors.

"It's never smart to keep the person who controls your destiny waiting."

"Destiny?" Liv asked.

"Okay, a little dramatic, but having the guidance counselor as one of the references for university applications is really good."

"First off, it's September, and second, you have lots of other people who'll say nice things about you."

"She's even offered to help me with filling out scholarship applications."

"Don't worry, your marks are good."

"My marks are *very* good," I corrected her and then realized how that sounded.

"Okay, so your marks are great."

"Not great, just very good. Great would be a ninety-seven or ninety-eight," I explained.

I was in the high eighties. That was good enough for some scholarship money, but I needed a full ride.

"And with all the studying you've been doing and prep work as well, you're going to ace your SATs. You've done really well on the practice tests."

"Practice tests are only practice tests, and the real tests are less than six weeks away. Which reminds me. Are you coming over on Saturday?"

"Can we do it Sunday instead?"

"I'm working at the nursing home."

I'd been doing volunteer work with seniors at the place where my mother worked. I liked helping, but mostly I was doing it to pad my college applications. Volunteer work went a long way with scholarship committees.

"Do you have something better to do on Saturday?" I asked.

"No. But I also know you really don't need to be doing so much," Liv said. "Besides your marks and the volunteer work at the nursing home, you're in the social justice club and the school band, and you're the manager of the boys' basketball team."

"I needed that athletic component on my application."

"Some of the guys are really hot."

"That's not why I'm doing it," I said.

"I know, but with all of that, do you really think you need to be hosting a new student?"

"Look, Mrs. Evans asked me, so I couldn't say no."

Liv grabbed me by the arm and pulled me to a stop. "You have another headache."

I realized I was rubbing one of my temples. "It's not bad."

I'd been having headaches on and off for a couple of years, but in the last six months they'd become so much worse. Some were so bad that I had to stay in bed.

"What did your doctor say?"

I'd just had another examination. "He said it's all in my head."

"Funny. What did he really say?"

"He said the MRI was good."

I'd had three MRIs over the last eighteen months. They didn't hurt or anything, but it was scary to slowly slide inside that big white and chrome machine. It felt like I was being eaten alive. There was nothing to do but lie there, trying not to move because that would spoil the image. Trying not to worry was even harder.

I had some medication to ease the pain, but I avoided it unless a headache was really bad. Today wasn't bad enough.

"Did they tell you again that you might be getting headaches because you're pushing yourself too hard?" Liv asked.

"I'm pushing myself as hard as I need to."

"Becky, do you really need to do this too?"

"What's so terrible about helping a new student feel welcome?"

"What do you know about the person you're hosting?" Liv said.

"He's from New York."

"That's a good start. Anybody from someplace else is better than somebody from here. The guys in this school seem to be only interested in fancy cars, basketball, hair products, and football."

"Wait, you *love* football and basketball."

"Of course I do. Everybody in Indiana loves the Colts and Pacers, but still, the guys here are so, well, *basic*."

"Don't you think you're simplifying things a little bit?" I asked.

"Do you think I'm wrong?"

I shrugged. It didn't matter. I didn't have time for any guy from here or from anyplace else. Not that I'd been beating them off with a stick.

I stopped at the door of the guidance office. "See you later."

Liv gave me a long hug, like she wasn't going to see me again.

"Could you take a picture of him and send it to me?" she asked.

"Goodbye, Liv."

There were four other people in the office, and I knew them all. That was no surprise since everybody in this town knew, or knew of, everybody else. My head was now throbbing a little harder. With my thumb and one finger of my left hand, I rubbed both temples. That was often enough to help.

Then I noticed that Mrs. Evans' door was closed. I looked at my watch. It was 8:32 — I was two minutes late; had they started without me? I walked over to knock, and the door popped open.

"Becky! Please come in," Mrs. Evans said.

She ushered me into her empty office. I took off my backpack and sat down as she took the seat behind her desk.

"Thank you so much for agreeing to do this."

"It's my pleasure."

"Our new student will be here in a few minutes." She leaned in closer. "There are things about him that I think you need to know."

Oh goodness, what was she going to say?

"And I need you to keep all of these things in the strictest of confidence."

"I will. I promise." What had I gotten myself into?

"This is a special situation, and we needed somebody special to make it work. Our principal specifically wants you to be the host. He said he's willing to put his name on your applications as well."

"That's great." Having both the guidance counselor and the principal was big.

"That means it's even more important that you really invest in this and do your best."

"I will. You know that."

"I do. Our new student is named Gene."

"I thought it was a guy."

"He is. Gene is spelled G-E-N-E. Now, what's so unusual is that he was homeschooled, so this isn't just his *new* school, this is his *first* school."

"Wow."

"Everything is going to be new and strange. And it's not like this is a small school."

We had more than 3,500 students, which made it one of the biggest in the state.

"I need you to stay very close to him, especially for the first week or two. I think he's going to need more than a host."

I'd agreed to be a host, and now it looked more like I was going to be a babysitter.

"He's going to be in three of your classes," Mrs. Evans said. "Since he's missed the first six weeks of school, I hope you could perhaps offer some tutoring if he needs it."

Which meant more time, more commitment, and more involvement. My mind spun around, looking for a way out, but there was none.

There was a knock on the door. Mrs. Evans called out, "Come in!" and the door started to open.

2

"YOU MUST BE Gene," Mrs. Evans said.

"Yes. I'm pleased to meet you, ma'am."

All I could see from my seat behind the door was part of a shiny metal briefcase peeking out from the door. What high school student carried a briefcase?

"Please come in and meet Becky James."

He came in. He was wearing a bright blue suit and his hair was longish and combed and parted off to the side. At least he matched his briefcase.

"I'm pleased to meet you, Becky," he said as he reached out and enthusiastically shook my hand. Between the clothes, the briefcase, and the handshake, it felt like I was meeting somebody a lot older — sort of like grandfather old.

He sat down. He had a big, goofy smile and bright, piercing eyes. He was good-looking, at least if you could look past the clothes and hair, and the expression.

"Did you have any trouble finding the guidance office?" Mrs. Evans asked.

"No, ma'am. I studied the floor plan of the school to help navigate the building."

"That's very, um, organized," Mrs. Evans said.

Strange was a better word.

"I imagine that being in our school is going to be very different for you," Mrs. Evans said.

"Yes, ma'am, very different."

"It's so unusual that you've never been in school before. Were your mother and father your teachers?" Mrs. Evans asked.

"Both my parents are doctors, and they assisted in my education along with a series of other instructors who had expertise in specific areas."

"Did you move here so that your parents could work at the hospital?" I asked.

"They are not medical doctors," Gene said. "My father has doctorates in genetics and physiology, and my mother has doctorates in both molecular biology and physics."

"That must make for some fascinating conversations around the dinner table," Mrs. Evans said.

"We talk very little at dinner. Mostly we read."

The bell sounded, and I jumped slightly. It was always too loud, and I felt it in my head. It always seemed more like it was waking the dead than signaling a class change.

"That's the warning bell, meaning you have five minutes to get to class," Mrs. Evans explained. "You have first period together, so Becky can bring you to class."

We got up as I took my backpack and Gene his briefcase. As Gene stepped out of the office, Mrs. Evans grabbed my arm. "Stay close, please, he's going to need your help more than any of us knew," she whispered.

I nodded, and she released my arm.

Gene was waiting at the guidance office door. He held it open for me, and I started down the hall.

"People do not seem to follow expected traffic flow patterns," he said.

"What?"

"In most of the world, traffic, both automobile and pedestrian, moves on the right side of the road or sidewalk."

"Oh, sure, I understand."

"Of course, in England and countries influenced by its previous colonization, such as India or Kenya, the pattern is —" Gene was bumped by a guy moving in the other direction.

"Nice briefcase," the guy said as he and his friends kept moving away.

"Thank you."

"He was being sarcastic," I said.

"Sarcastic?"

"You don't know what sarcasm is?"

"Sarcasm is the use of irony to mock or convey contempt, but why would I be the subject of it?"

"Do you see anybody else carrying a briefcase?"

He stopped walking and looked around in all directions, like he was doing a survey. "There are no other briefcases. Tomorrow I will have a backpack."

And you might want to lose the suit as well, I thought but didn't say.

Moving along, a couple more times people bumped in to Gene. He might have known the floor plan of the school, but he didn't seem to know how to walk amongst people. I guessed there weren't big crowds when you were homeschooled.

We came up to our room, and I took a seat at the front. Biology was one of the classes I found most difficult, and I had to soak in anything I could, sort of like osmosis — which is a pretty good biology term. Mr. Benjamin was at his desk, head down, marking.

Gene stood beside my desk.

I gestured to the open spot beside me. Gene slid into the seat. He clicked open his briefcase and pulled out a notepad and two pens. I liked that he had two pens. I always had two pens. I'd probably found the only thing we had in common.

The PA came to life, and we all stood for the anthem and the pledge of allegiance and then settled back into our seats.

"Okay, everybody," Mr. Benjamin said. "We're having a surprise quiz."

There was a collective groan from across the room. I wasn't happy about the test but happy that I'd spent some time last night doing a review. I was ready, but what about Gene?

Mr. Benjamin started handing out the tests to the person in the front desk of each row. "Pass them to the back."

"Sir, there's a problem," I said as he handed me the tests to pass back. "We have a new student."

Mr. Benjamin looked at Gene. "I'm not sure how I didn't notice you in that suit."

"I'm his host," I explained. "Should he go to the library or cafeteria while we take the test?"

"Oh, no, he'll take the test."

"But he hasn't been in class."

"The test will show me what he doesn't know. What's your name?"

"Gene Newman, sir, and I want to take the test."

"Well, Gene Newman, you are definitely going to take the test." He handed him a stack of tests, and Gene took one, turned, and passed the others back.

I leaned closer to Gene. "Don't worry."

He responded with a smile and then looked down at the test.

I WAS ALMOST halfway through page two when Gene got to his feet. He walked to Mr. Benjamin's desk and handed him the test. I'd caught sight of him working away, but now I assumed he'd just given up. I understood. My recurring nightmare was being handed a test and looking down and the words were all written in a foreign language. Funny, the more I studied for my SATs, the more often that dream came to me. Maybe I really was putting too much pressure on myself.

Gene offered me another smile as he returned to his seat. He really did have a nice smile. Okay, I didn't have time for this — I needed to get back to the test.

3

I LOOKED UP as Gene walked into the cafeteria. He stood out like a beacon. After biology, I'd walked with him to calculus second period before I went off to music and he had physics. Moving between classes, we were the center of comments, looks, laughs, and smiles.

"There's your new BFF," Liv said.

Sasha and Emma turned around to look.

"Wow, that suit's even brighter in person," Sasha said.

"I thought it was some sort of filter effect in the pictures, but it's real," Emma added.

"You've all seen pictures of him?" I asked.

"There have been tweets, Instagram pictures, and I've got three separate WhatsApp messages about him and you," Liv said.

"Me?"

"You're in the pictures."

"And look, he's carrying his little briefcase!" Emma exclaimed. "That's so cute."

"He's actually cute himself if you can get past the clothes, briefcase, and hair," Liv said. "You should ask him to join us."

"Yeah, invite him over," Emma said, and Sasha nodded in agreement.

Before I could answer, Gene yelled out my name from across the cafeteria and waved.

I waved back. As he came toward us, I saw there were lots of eyes on him, and more than a few phones came out and more pictures were taken. Liv looked amused. I felt embarrassed for him and for me.

"Hello, Becky. May I have permission to dine with you and your friends?"

"Of course you can," Liv answered. "I'm Becky's best friend, Liv."

"And we're Emma and Sasha. And you have to be Gene."

"Yes, Gene Newman." He shook hands with all of them in that awkward way he had about him. He sat down, opened his briefcase, and pulled out a huge paper bag.

"So, Gene Newman, how are you enjoying your first day?" Liv asked.

"Becky has been most helpful."

"Although not helpful in getting you out of that surprise test," I said. "It was wrong that you had to take it when you haven't even covered the material."

"It was all right. I enjoyed taking the test."

Liv, Sasha, and Emma all exchanged looks of surprise.

Gene started to take things out of his bag. There was a big bottle of water, a gigantic bag of cut-up vegetables, two bananas, an apple, four protein bars, and a yogurt.

"That's quite a lunch," I said.

"I don't see any meat," Sasha said. "Are you a vegetarian?"

"Yes."

"For how long?" Liv asked.

"For my entire life."

"Is there a reason for it?" Emma asked.

"I believe that eating meat is wrong."

I tried to hide my burger with my arm.

"Not that I judge those who choose to eat meat," he said.

Had he seen me do that? Of course not — he hardly realized anything that was going on around him.

"You might be the only vegetarian in the school," Liv said.

"He might be the only vegetarian in all of Nobleton," I added.

"Gene, would you like some of my vegetarian meal?" Liv asked as she slid her plate of French fries toward him.

"No, thank you. I do not eat fast food."

"You've *never* had a French fry?" Liv asked.

"No."

"And being a vegetarian would mean that you've never had a Big Mac?"

"That is a hamburger from McDonald's, correct?"

"Well, yeah," Liv said. "You make it sound like you've never even been to a McDonald's."

"I have never been to any fast-food place."

Liv looked at me. "Did you say he was from New York or Mars?"

"Mars would be an impossibility given the technology that is —"

"Gene, she's joking. He's from a little place in upstate New York."

"Plattsburgh."

"No matter how little it is, it must have some fast-food places," Liv said.

"We lived outside of town."

"Then living in this town must be very different for you," I said.

"Where exactly do you live?" Liv asked.

"We live on a property over on the south side of town, 170 Chambers."

"Wait, that's Sarah's old place," Liv said.

"I am unaware who the previous resident was."

"It's a three-story green house with white trim surrounded by big trees, right?" I asked.

"Yes."

"We used to spend a lot of time there," Liv explained.

"It belonged to a good friend of ours," Emma added.

"She moved away?"

"A few years ago. It all happened really quickly because her mother got a big job in California. It happened so fast that they even left most of their furniture behind."

"The house came with furnishings," Gene confirmed.

"They rented it out, but I think the place has been vacant for the last year or two," Liv added.

"I'm curious, which room is yours?" I asked.

"It is up on the third floor."

"Do you have a big tree outside your bedroom window?"

"Yes, right beside my window."

"He's in Sarah's old room!" Emma exclaimed.

I looked down and suddenly realized my clarinet wasn't there. I fumbled around looking beneath the table and couldn't find it. I jumped to my feet. "I have to go back to the music room. I forgot my clarinet."

"You know, people leave their instruments in the music room all the time," Liv said.

"I used to leave my trombone in the music room back closet

sometimes," Emma said.

"First off, nobody wants to steal a trombone, and second, didn't you end up losing your instrument?" Sasha asked.

"Yeah, but that was because I forgot it on the school bus, not in the music room."

"I'm going to get my clarinet." I grabbed my backpack.

"Can I come with you?" Gene asked.

"You can stay here and eat. It's really not that exciting or ..." I stopped myself. He looked sad and alone. He really didn't have a friend in this place. "Sure, if you want to."

"Thank you."

Liv shot me a look that sort of said, *How strange.*

Gene quickly put the remains of his lunch back into his briefcase.

"See you later, Liv, Emma, Sasha."

"Nice to meet you, Gene Newman," Sasha said.

"It was nice to meet all of you." He shook each of their hands once again.

It was obvious we were being watched as we crossed the caf, and I could see smirks and hear laughs. Gene didn't seem to notice.

"What do you think of your first day so far?" I asked as we reached the hall.

"It has been overwhelming in some ways."

When he said that, he looked like a lost little boy hiding beneath his suit, and I suddenly felt guilty. I hadn't even offered for him to have lunch with me.

"There are so many people, and everything is loud. I do not think I fit in that well."

I laughed before I could stop myself.

"I know I am different. Tomorrow I will do better."

"As I said, start by ditching the briefcase." I felt bad for saying that. "I didn't mean to hurt your feelings."

"You were just relaying that information."

"I guess it's sort of my job."

"Thank you for volunteering to do this job."

Really, though, I hadn't volunteered. If Mrs. Evans hadn't approached me, I never would have done this.

"There is just so much new information to process," he said.

This couldn't be easy. Along with everything else, here on his first day, he'd had to take a surprise test. I felt sorry for him.

The music room door was closed. I wondered if it was locked with my clarinet inside. I turned the knob. It was open, the lights off and the room empty. I flipped on the lights, and the fluorescent tubes hummed to life. I looked around and there it was, right under the chair where I'd been sitting. I rushed over and picked the case up. It felt heavy, like the instrument was inside. I put the case down, opened it, and there it was. I let out a sigh of relief.

"How long have you played?" Gene asked.

"I started in seventh grade. So about five years."

"You must be very good."

"Well, I don't know about very good, but I'm in the school band."

"Can anybody be in the band?"

"Anybody can try out. Why, do you play an instrument?" I asked.

He hesitated for a second before answering. "What is your favorite instrument?"

"Even though I don't play it, it's the saxophone."

He smiled. "I play the saxophone."

"Alto, tenor, or soprano?" I asked.

"All three. Do you have a favorite saxophone player?"

"I guess I'd go with the classics. You know, Charlie Parker, Stan Getz, and, of course, Grover Washington Junior."

"I like them too."

There was something about the way he said that, something about him saying he played the saxophone, that just didn't seem right. Did he really play? There was one sure way to find out.

I looked around. There was a saxophone sitting on a stand in the corner. Obviously, some people had a lot more confidence than I did that their instruments were safe here. I walked over to the instrument. It still had a mouthpiece in place. I picked it up and brought it over.

"Play something for me." I went to hand it to him, and he backed off like I was trying to hand him a poisonous snake.

"It is not mine. I will play for you, but with my saxophone."

Again, more suspicions rose. I needed to push this a little bit further.

"Why didn't you sign up for music as a class?"

"I could change and do that."

"Maybe you should," I said, although I suddenly felt bad for pushing him, especially if this was all a lie. I'd give him a way out.

"It's hard to change courses. Besides, it's really difficult to enroll in an advanced instrumental music course. You basically have to audition because being in the class puts you in the school band."

I returned the saxophone to the stand and then closed my clarinet case and started out of the room, with Gene right behind me. This all felt awkward. I'd change the subject.

"So, what brought your family to Nobleton? Was it because of your parents' work?"

"They moved here *with* their work. They have a full laboratory in our basement to continue their research."

"A lab in the basement makes it sound like Dr. Frankenstein, or I guess Doctors Frankenstein since there's two of them."

He looked confused.

"You know, the famous book by Mary Shelley about the mad scientist who created life in his basement?"

"Life cannot be created, although the genome can be reconfigured."

"Um, sure, thanks for sharing that."

"You are welcome."

The hallway was starting to fill up. I suddenly became more aware of the clanking of the lockers, the loud voices, the laughter, the discussions and arguments going on. It was loud. We wove our way around knots of students, people sitting on the floor, leaning against their lockers, legs sticking out into the hall. A couple of the guys were tossing a football, and two more of them were wrestling. One smashed the other into a locker with a loud, metallic thud. There was music coming from little stereo systems in different lockers. This was noisy, crowded, and chaotic. No wonder Gene was finding it off-putting.

"What sort of research are your parents doing?" I asked over the noise.

"It would be difficult to explain. In fact, I am not allowed to explain very much of it."

"You make it sound like it's top secret government stuff," I joked.

He leaned in close and lowered his voice. "I cannot confirm or deny that."

What a strange answer — or, really, a non-answer. "It sounds like they must be very interesting people."

"Would you like to meet them? They told me I could invite my new friends over. You are my friend, right?"

There was a pleading quality to his voice, a look in his eyes. I realized I was his only friend in the school, maybe in the whole state.

"Would I have to sign a secret agreement if I came over?" I joked.

"No. Probably not. When do you want to come over?"

"I don't know exactly. I have band practice and volunteer work, and I'm going to be managing the boys' basketball team, and that's going to start soon. And I've got extra studying that I'm doing to prepare to get into university."

He looked like a puppy dog who had been scolded.

"No, I really do want to come over. I just have to check my schedule. Speaking of which, what class is next for you?"

"I have chemistry, and you go to English."

"Yes, I do. How do you know that?"

"I saw it when your binder was open in biology. After your English class we both have American history, then you go to P.E. while I have economics, and your day ends with Spanish and I have computer studies."

"I feel like I'm being stalked," I said.

"Oh, no, I would never do that."

"I was just joking."

The bell sounded to signal the end of lunch.

"Okay, I'm off to English. See you in American history — I'll save you a seat."

"Thank you for being my guide, Becky."

He offered his hand, and we shook hands again. Was he going to do that all the time? I'd have to talk to him about that.

4

MR. BENJAMIN HAD our tests marked and started to hand them back to us.

He handed me mine. "Excellent work by Becky."

There, at the top of the page in red ink, was a large *91*. It was good, but not really excellent.

"But Becky's not our top mark. And with a ninety-three is Colby." He handed him his paper.

Colby looked pretty happy. We had an unofficial, unstated competition going on, and he'd won this round.

"But neither of those are the top mark," Mr. Benjamin said as he held up another paper.

I was surprised. Colby looked over at me. He looked surprised too. Who could have — "Our top mark belongs to our newest student, Gene, with a ninety-seven."

"What?" I gasped.

People all looked as stunned and surprised as I felt. Then somebody started clapping, and others joined in.

Gene looked unaware of what he'd just done. The guy who hadn't studied, hadn't read anything, hadn't been in class the first six weeks of the term, hadn't even been in the *state*, had the highest mark.

"It looks like Becky and Colby are going to have to step up

their game," Mr. Benjamin said as he continued to hand out tests. "Maybe you're all going to have to work harder."

"Or maybe we should stop studying and going to class if we want higher marks," Sam chimed in from the back of the room.

"Do you really want to test that theory?" Mr. Benjamin asked.

Sam pretended to zip his mouth closed.

Gene didn't say anything. It was like he didn't even have a hint that this was something special. Or how it could be annoying. He just didn't know.

I was just glad that he was here this morning. After his first day, Gene hadn't returned the next. I'd been worried it was all too much for him and he wasn't coming back. And if that was the case, would Mrs. Evans blame me for not doing my job well enough?

When I'd first seen him in the hall this morning, he'd run up to say hello to me. I was relieved and happy to see him, but he was so happy he was practically jumping up and down. If he had a tail, he would have been wagging it. It was embarrassing and uncomfortable and, well, sort of nice. Other than Liv, who was ever that happy to see me?

I was also happy that he wasn't in his bright blue suit. He was, however, wearing brown leisure pants, something my grandfather would have worn. He now had a backpack instead of a briefcase. He'd taken that piece of advice.

The bell sounded, and people got to their feet and started scrambling away, leaving Mr. Benjamin in mid-sentence. He stopped talking and walked over to where Gene and I still sat.

"I don't know how you did that," he said to Gene.

"The test was fairly straightforward, referencing common

knowledge, and the answers seemed to make logical sense in most cases."

"Thank you, I try to make my tests fair. And, Becky, you did very well."

"I studied and read the textbook."

"It shows. Good work. I guess you're two of my stars," Mr. Benjamin said. "Just think, Gene was one question away from perfect."

I got up. "I better get him to his next class."

Gene got up and shook Mr. Benjamin's hand. I really had to talk to him about that.

Some of the class was hanging out just outside the door, talking. There were a few comments to Gene about his test. Sam, always being Sam, offered to sit beside him during the next test and he could help Gene by "sharing" answers. Gene didn't get the attempted joke.

We started walking. "It's just unbelievable that you could get a ninety-seven."

"No, I did. Look," Gene said as he offered me his test.

"I'm not questioning that it *did* happen. It's just hard for me to believe you could do that without studying or at least being in class."

He was still holding the test in his hand, the big red *97* very visible. "How about if you stop waving that around and you put it away."

He flipped his backpack around and slipped the test into the side pocket.

"By the way, nice backpack."

"I saw many people carrying this model on my first day, so I thought it would help me blend in," Gene explained.

"It helps." Should I mention the clothes? Maybe not yet. "It's pretty amazing that you were one answer away from perfect."

"I could have gotten perfect."

"What do you mean?"

"I wrote an answer that I believed Mr. Benjamin would mark incorrect even though it was actually correct."

"So, you know the right answer, and Mr. Benjamin, who wrote the test, doesn't?" I asked.

"I have done fairly extensive independent research in this area. Do you think I should inform Mr. Benjamin about his incorrect answer?"

"I think you'd better leave it alone. You have enough people annoyed with you already," I said.

"Why would anybody be annoyed with me?"

"Because you got a higher mark than all of us who studied, attended class, and did the reading. It makes everybody else feel like they aren't smart."

"You had the third highest mark."

"I studied. You didn't. I just can't get over how you did that."

He shrugged. "It was not a hard test."

"Don't say that so loud."

We entered calculus class. As usual, I headed to the front. My new shadow followed behind and took the vacant seat to my right, just like he had in biology. I was certainly going to see a whole lot of him over the months to come. I just had to hope we weren't going to have a surprise calculus test today.

THE BELL SOUNDED to signal the end of period two. There was no test, but Gene had shown his stuff. He had volunteered answers to questions, and he was always right. He and Mrs. Matthews had gotten into a detailed discussion about some obscure mathematical theory that only they knew anything about. It was a little bit like watching two people talking in a foreign language.

"I'll see you later," I said as I headed out the door. My music room was in one direction, and Gene's physics class was in the other.

"You will definitely see me," he replied.

I had to hope he'd start to make a few friends. Or was part of my job trying to get him friends? Mrs. Evans really owed me a great reference for doing this.

"I have to go to my locker before my next class," he said.

"Then you'd better hurry, or you'll be late."

He hurried off.

Walking through the hall by myself, I suddenly realized how much I enjoyed being alone. Gene was nice, and innocent, and obviously bizarrely smart, but it felt more like childcare than hosting. It was funny how he knew so much about school subjects but so little about life. I'd tried to get him talking about regular things. He didn't watch television, didn't have a favorite movie or song, and didn't know anything about sports. It would be good to be in music and not have to struggle to make conversation with him.

I happily settled into my seat and pulled out my clarinet. All around, other students assembled their instruments, playing scales or snippets of songs, waiting for class to formally begin. Funny how, thanks to Gene, I seemed to be more aware of the sounds of the school.

I looked up. Gene was standing at the door, and in his one hand was a saxophone case. I was surprised. No, I was shocked. Part of me had really believed that he didn't play the saxophone, that he was just trying to impress me, and now here he was, carrying a saxophone.

I got to my feet, still carrying my clarinet, and rushed over.

"You can't just walk into a class and join. It's not like home-schooling, you have to follow your timetable."

"I changed my timetable so I could be in music instead of physics."

"But why would you do that?"

"You said, 'Just out of curiosity. If you play the saxophone, why didn't you take music?'"

"That doesn't mean that I thought you should drop out of physics and sign up for music!"

"Should I sign back up for physics?" he asked.

"You should do what you want to do."

"Then I want to be in music."

"Okay, but are you good enough to be in the school band?"

"I believe I am."

I suddenly realized all the instruments had gone silent. All eyes were on us, including those of Ms. Freeman, who was standing at the front, waiting and listening.

"I'm assuming you must be my *potential* new student, Gene Newman."

"Yes, ma'am."

"I was informed by the office about you," Ms. Freeman said. "You are aware that to be part of an advanced music class, a student has to audition to show they can perform at this level?"

"Yes. Mrs. Evans informed me of that. Would you like me to play now?"

"Gene, you don't have to do this," I said.

"He does if he wants to be in this class," Ms. Freeman said. "Can one of the alto sax players give him a piece of music to play?" she added. "Something *challenging*. Becky, why don't you help your new friend to get a music stand and a seat out front, where everybody can hear and see him."

I wanted to argue with her, to protect him, the way I should have protected him from the biology test — wait, he got a ninety-seven on the test. But this was different. It didn't matter if he could play the saxophone, he'd have to be amazing to see a difficult piece of music for the first time and play it perfectly. Especially with all these people staring at him. This was less like an audition and more like a public execution.

I put the stand in front of him as he opened up his case. "You don't have to do this," I whispered again. "You can play for me later, when I come to your house."

"I have to play for Ms. Freeman if I wish to get into the class."

He pulled his saxophone out. It was beautiful and looked brand new — like it had never been played before. Glenn, one of the sax players, put a piece of music on the stand.

"Good luck, man, this one's really hard. I've been working on it for the last two weeks."

"Thank you," Gene replied. He slung the instrument around his neck and adjusted the strap slightly.

"Would you like to look the piece over first?" Ms. Freeman asked.

"No, that will not be necessary, ma'am."

"Can he warm up, practice the piece in the hall for a few minutes?" I asked.

"That would be fair," Ms. Freeman replied.

Her voice had softened. She must have realized that it wasn't right to have him —

"That will not be necessary either, ma'am."

He put the sax to his lips and started playing. The first few notes were clear and round — he was playing, and he was playing well. I recognized the piece. It was part of our band repertoire, and the sax had a solo part. It was a very complicated part, and Glenn and the other two sax players hadn't been able to play well enough for us to do it in performance. I also knew that the piece got progressively harder. Would he be able to keep it up? Then again, even if he didn't, he'd already proved that he could play. He was really good, better than the other sax players in the class. His tone was wonderful. He was playing with such feeling, such emotion.

And then I realized how stupid I had been to think he'd lied about playing to try to impress me. Thank goodness I hadn't mentioned that idea to anybody. Liv would have never let me hear the end of it.

He came to the hardest part of the piece, and he was hitting the notes perfectly. He had great timing, even better tone, and a real feel for the music. Note by note, he was doing it, and then he started playing it differently. I realized he was transposing the notes and playing them half an octave higher. Then he started double-tonguing the notes! It was unbelievable.

He suddenly morphed into another song: it was Grover Washington, his most famous song — "Just the Two of Us." It sounded so much like Grover that if I didn't know better, I would have thought I was listening to a recording.

He stopped playing. There was silence. It was like nobody knew how to react. Then Ms. Freeman began cheering and clapping, and everybody else started clapping wildly. She rushed over and threw her arms around him and gave him a big hug. I had to assume that he'd passed the audition and was in the class and in the band.

5

I CAME OUT of the coach's office. He'd been explaining to me the jobs I'd do as the manager. At different nets around the gym there were guys putting up shots, playing horse, or having little games of two on two or three on three.

I looked up, and across the gym was the last thing I expected to see: Gene sitting in the bleachers. He gave me a little wave, got up, and started across the gym, straight toward me, not noticing that he was walking directly through one of the games.

"What are you doing here?" I asked.

"I thought an apology was in order."

"Oh, yeah." Somehow, he'd realized that I had doubted his ability to play the saxophone.

"I wanted to apologize for showing up in music class without asking your permission."

I hadn't seen that coming. "You didn't need my permission."

"I wanted it to be a surprise."

"I was surprised, especially at how well you played."

"Surprised? I told you I could play."

This was my chance to apologize to him. I didn't. It was too embarrassing to say I'd thought he was making the whole thing up to impress me.

"I don't think I've ever seen Ms. Freeman so excited about somebody joining the band."

Gene suddenly shot out his hand and grabbed a ball as it came toward my head. I jumped backward and shrieked a little.

"Sorry, Becky!" Devon yelled as he trotted over. He was a senior and one of the returning stars of our basketball team, so for him the tryouts were just going to be a formality.

"Good reflexes," he said to Gene. "Can you shoot?"

"At the net?" Gene asked, nodding toward the near basket.

Devon laughed. "No, that net." He pointed to the one on the other side of the gym. The other three guys who had been playing with Devon were now standing there, watching and listening. Once again, Gene was the center of attention, but not the kind anybody wanted.

Gene turned so he was squarely facing the basket.

"He's just kidding," I explained.

Still holding his sax case in his left hand, Gene, underhanded, tossed the ball up into the air. It was a long, arcing shot that rose up and up and then down before dropping into the far net.

The four guys exploded, laughing and jumping up and down and hooting.

"Unbelievable! He made it with a granny shot!" Devon yelled as he slapped Gene on the back. "Can you do that again?"

Gene shrugged.

"Get him the ball!" Devon ordered.

One of the guys tossed Devon the ball, and he handed it to Gene. "Go ahead, try."

Once again, Gene studied the net. I got the feeling he was doing

some sort of complex mathematical equation in his head, thinking through the angle, arc, and coefficient of the toss. After seeing
him in calculus class, maybe he was.

He pulled back the ball and threw it. Smoothly, slightly rotating, it rose into the air, reached the top of its arc, and then came
down, hit the rim, bounced up, and then missed.

Again, everybody hooted and hollered.

"Not bad, not bad, man," Devon said.

One of the other guys, Ethan, joined us. "That is so old school,
granny-shot old school!"

He and Devon exchanged a high five.

"You're the guy with the blue suit, right?" Devon asked.

"Yes, I own a blue suit."

"Did you play on your old school's team?" Devon asked.

I laughed. "His old school didn't have a basketball team, or any
other teams. He was homeschooled."

"You might want to try out for our school team. There's no telling when we might need a full-court granny shot," Ethan added.

Gene turned to me. "Sarcasm?"

I nodded.

"You might even have an in with the team because Becky is the
manager."

"Maybe you two should go back to playing ball," I suggested.

I took Gene by the arm and walked him out of the gym. The
sound of the bouncing balls, squeaking shoes, and yelling faded
behind.

"Don't let them bother you," I said.

"They seem nice."

"Actually, they are. They're both good guys, but you know how guys are, always giving each other a hard time."

He looked like he didn't know, but then, how would he? It wasn't like there was anybody around to give him any sort of time. I was starting to wonder if he ever hung out with people or played sports in the community.

"What does the manager of the basketball team do?" Gene asked.

"I fill out forms, arrange for us to be in tournaments, fill out the score sheets, make sure we have refs and minor officials, and put things away. Things like that."

"Are you there for all the games?"

"And all the practices and all the upcoming tryouts to determine who makes the team."

"When are the tryouts?"

"They start two weeks from now on a Monday morning. Do you even play ball?"

"You saw me shoot."

"I saw you take a lucky shot in a strange way. Do you *like* basketball?"

"Definitely."

"Who's your favorite player?"

He shrugged. "Michael Jordan is very good, right?"

"He *was* the best player in the game — until he retired almost twenty years ago. So, are the Bulls your favorite team?"

"Yes, the Bulls."

"Everybody I know *hates* the Bulls. You live in Indiana now, so you should know the correct answer to that question is the Pacers."

"They are a good team as well. You believed I was not able to play the saxophone, correct?"

I felt like I was caught. Time to confess, apologize — or lie some more. "I didn't think you could play that well. You were amazing!"

"I have not been playing that long."

"That's impossible. You were spectacular."

"I learn things quickly," Gene said. "Very quickly. And I like basketball."

"But can you play well enough to try out for the team?"

He smiled but didn't answer.

6

"HOW ARE YOU girls doing?" my mother asked as she walked into my room, where Liv and I were studying. She was carrying a tray with cold drinks, cheese, crackers, and some sliced-up fruit.

"I thought you were doing a double shift today."

"A single this morning, and then back for an overnight. You're volunteering tomorrow, as usual, aren't you?"

"A few hours in the morning. I was wondering, with Dad working now, couldn't you cut back your hours?"

"We still have some catching up to do."

I knew they'd dipped into my college fund to pay bills, and they were working to put back the money. I was working hard so they wouldn't have to.

"Thanks for the snacks, Mrs. J," Liv said. "It almost makes up for your daughter lying to me."

"Becky, are you lying to your friend?" my mother asked.

"Of course not!"

"Yes, she is. She said that the more we studied, the easier these practice tests were going to get," Liv said.

"It has gotten easier!" I protested.

"Then why did I score less on this test than the last one?"

"Sometimes the tests have specific questions that you don't know. On average, you're scoring almost seventy points higher than you did in the beginning. We both are scoring higher."

"You more than me," Liv said.

I was up 127 points. At 1340, I was just above the 90th percentile. For most people, that was what they were aiming for. I wanted at least another 30 points.

"How do you think your boyfriend would do on the SATs?" Liv asked.

"Who exactly are you talking about?" I asked as my mother's ears perked up.

"I think she means Gene, because you do talk about him a lot," my mother said.

I shot her a dirty look.

"Well, well, well, who's obsessed with who, is the question," Liv said.

"I'm not obsessed. But you have to admit that being around him is like watching a three-legged dog run."

"More like a two-headed frog," Liv said.

"Maybe both," I said. "He has twice the brains but is so awkward at the same time."

"Maybe I should invite him for dinner," my mother suggested.

"What a wonderful idea!" Liv exclaimed. "Can I come as well?"

"You know you're always welcome to join us for —"

"No, she can't!" I said, cutting my mother off.

Liv slowly shook her head. "Will you at least tell me about it afterwards?"

"If she doesn't, then I will," my mother said.

"Whose side are you on?"

"I'm on nobody's side. I just want to meet him."

"Gene is innocent. He's, well, sort of sweet," I said.

"Admirable qualities for a pet," Liv said.

"Not a pet. More like my pet project."

"I still can't believe he transferred to music to be close to you," Liv said.

"That wasn't why he transferred." I had to hope that wasn't why he'd transferred. "He's an incredible saxophone player."

"Yeah, I read the comments on Instagram. Somebody even posted a twenty-second video of him playing. And I can't wait to see if he shows up for the basketball tryouts," Liv said.

"He doesn't strike me as a basketball player," I said.

"So, tell me, what's it like having your own personal stalker?"

"Gene is not a stalker."

"Isn't he? He changed classes to be close to you, he's now in the band, he's threatening to try out for the basketball team, and he follows you around the school like a lost puppy."

"That does sound a bit like a stalker to me," my mother said.

"He has nobody else, and he's scared."

"You've always had a soft spot for lost animals," my mother said.

"You know, Mrs. J, you better be careful about having him for dinner. If you feed a dog, you'll never get rid of it."

"How about if we just go back to studying now?" I suggested.

"Nibble first," my mother said.

"And then how about after we finish the snack, we go for a walk?" Liv suggested. "I need to clear my head and stretch my legs."

IT WAS LATE afternoon, but it was still much hotter than we usually got in late September. There was a beautiful breeze that was wafting the scent of harvested crops from the fields beyond the edges of the town. It was quiet, and there were more little kids on bikes on the sidewalks than cars on the streets. Tall trees lined the avenues, and every lawn was well maintained and every flower bed well tended. On the porches of many houses, people sat, having a cool drink and just enjoying the warm weather. As we passed, we were offered a greeting, an exchange, or at least a nod of a head. We knew almost everybody. It was safe and reassuring and peaceful and stifling and suffocating all at once.

"Turn this way," Liv said as we came to a corner.

Any way was as good as any other, so I was happy to let her decide.

"When we graduate from high school and go away, are you going to miss living here?" I asked.

"Sometimes I don't want to leave, and other times I can't wait to go."

"I feel the same way. It's so peaceful that, well, it's —"

"Boring," Liv said. "When was the last time anything new happened in this town? Well, at least before your boyfriend moving in."

"Please stop calling him my boyfriend."

"My apologies. Your stalker. Why can't I get a stalker?"

"He's yours if you want him."

"Are you admitting that he's yours to give up?" Liv asked.

"Who knows? Maybe he's sitting with us at lunch because it's you he's trying to get close to."

"Becky, he only has puppy dog eyes for you. It's you he's interested in."

"You're wrong."

"I know one way to find out. Why don't we knock on his door and ask if he wants to come out to play?" she suggested.

I suddenly realized that we were only a block away from Gene's street.

"You had this planned all along, didn't you?" I asked.

"I always like to have a destination. You should appreciate that more than anybody else I know. So, what do you think?"

"You want us to just knock on his door?"

"Or ring the doorbell," Liv suggested.

"And just who's the stalker?"

"We'd only be stalkers if we just walked by or hid in the bushes, so let's go and call on him."

We turned on to his street, which was on the edge of the town. This was the last street before the farms and fields took over completely.

"The trees are so much bigger now," Liv said.

"It's been almost four years since we've been here."

We came up to the property. The hedge was high and untended. Through the gaps, we could see that the grass hadn't been cut, and the house, which was well back from the road, was surrounded by tall weeds.

"Apparently Gene's parents aren't much into gardening," Liv said.

"They just moved in," I replied, defending them. "And it has been deserted for a long time."

"Well?" Liv asked as she opened the gate.

I hesitated. I was also nervous, but what choice did I have? I stepped through the gate, and Liv followed.

The house was three stories high with a weather vane and lightning rods at the tops of the steep peaks, gingerbread at the eaves, and old wooden windows with shutters. Paint was peeling, one of those shutters hung on an angle, and the porch railing was missing more than a few spindles. We always used to joke that it looked like it was haunted.

"Do you think this is a good idea?" Liv asked.

"It was your idea!"

"I wasn't arguing about whose idea it was, just questioning whether it was a good one."

"Sometimes you drive me —"

The front door opened, and Gene appeared. He was in the shortest little shorts and brown loafers and a shirt that was too small. He was holding a basketball.

"Wow," Liv said under her breath. "The guy is built."

I was thinking the same thing exactly. He was rock solid, and his muscles showed through the tight shirt.

He hadn't noticed us. He started dribbling the basketball as he crossed the porch, went down the side steps, and walked onto the driveway. He looked completely focused — and was he talking to himself?

I cleared my throat, and he looked over and skidded to a stop. He looked stunned. He stared at us, and his face tilted to one side like he was trying to process what he was seeing.

"Hey, Gene!" I called out, breaking the silence, trying to sound casual and enthusiastic all at one time.

"Yeah, how you doing?" Liv added.

"Well," he said. "I did not expect either of you. Or anybody, really."

"We came to see if you wanted to come and get an ice cream with us," Liv said.

"Ice cream with the two of you?"

He sounded genuinely confused.

"It doesn't have to be an ice cream," Liv said. "It could be a soda, or you could just come along and get nothing. Would you like to go with us?"

"Yes, an ice cream would be good. I have to ask permission. Excuse me." He turned and went back into the house, leaving us standing in front of the porch.

"That was strange," Liv said. "But now we know that Gene is a hottie. I didn't see that coming at all."

Before I could reply, the door opened again, and Gene reappeared.

"Please come in. My parents want to meet you ... both of you."

7

HE GESTURED FOR us to come in.

"Unbelievable," Liv said, her voice barely a whisper.

I knew what she was talking about. The furniture, the carpet on the floor, and even the pictures on the walls were the same as the last time we'd stood here.

"Nothing has changed," I said.

"The house came with everything," Gene explained.

"What furniture is in your room?" Liv asked.

"It's all white with a big —"

"Brass headboard," I said, cutting him off.

He nodded. "You mentioned the tree before," Gene said. "It is a black walnut tree."

"We used to climb that tree," Liv said. "We'd climb right to the top and right into —"

"Right to the top," I said, cutting her off.

The basement door opened. Two people appeared — a man and a woman — both wearing lab coats. They closed the door with a loud clank. It was a heavy metal door with a big keypad by the handle. That was definitely new and made me curious about just what was going on in that lab.

"These are my parents," Gene said. "My mother, Dr. Lawrence, and my father, Dr. Wilson."

His mother took off her glasses, and his father put his on. They were looking at us — no, they were looking at *me*. I felt like I was being studied. I was taller than either of them, and Gene towered over all of us. These were his parents?

"You are Becky," his mother said.

"Yes. And this is —"

"Your best friend, Liv," his father said.

"Gene told you about us?" Liv asked.

"Gene keeps us fully informed of his daily school activities and interactions."

Somehow that didn't sound like a casual "What did you do in school today?" sort of thing.

"How scientific," Liv said.

"We are scientists," his father said, and his mother nodded.

"Becky, we appreciate you helping Gene to navigate the uncharted waters of high school," his mother said. "We can be of limited assistance in that area, as I was only ten years old when I entered ninth grade."

"And I never attended high school at all," his father added. "I went from eighth grade to university."

Okay, this explained more about Gene being so smart.

"Becky, you and Gene share biology, calculus, music, and American history," his father said.

"And don't forget they're in the band together," Liv said. "Gene and I take chemistry."

"Yes, we are aware. Chemistry is not one of your strengths," his mother said.

I almost laughed but contained myself.

"Becky, you are very healthy looking," his father said.

That was such a strange thing to say, and I could see Liv working not to laugh.

"Thanks, I guess."

"Please excuse my partner," his wife said. "He can be a little socially obtuse."

One more way that he was their kid.

"Perhaps in exchange for you helping to guide Gene through the mystery of high school he could offer to tutor you in some subjects," his father suggested.

"Becky is one of the top students in the school," Liv replied. "Her marks are about a ninety average."

"Ah, so the standards are lower," his father said, and his mother nodded in agreement.

I thought Liv and I and the whole school had just been insulted.

"Come to think about it, that is a great offer for Gene to help Becky!" Liv exclaimed. I could see a look in her eyes — a combination of amusement and mischief — that none of them could see or understand.

"We were studying for our SATs today. Have you started prepping for them?" I asked Gene.

"I'm not sure what SATs are."

"You don't know about SATs?" Liv asked. She sounded astonished.

He shook his head.

"They're standardized tests that help to determine if you qualify for post-secondary education," his mother explained.

"Did you take them?" Gene asked his mother.

"We both did," his father said.

"Just out of curiosity, what did you two score on the test?" Liv asked.

"I scored fifteen-ninety," his father answered.

"That's almost perfect," I said.

"I scored sixteen hundred," his mother replied.

"That *is* perfect," I gasped.

"Overall, the questions were remarkably unchallenging," his mother continued.

"The most challenging part was providing an answer that would satisfy the requirement of what is believed to be correct rather than providing an alternate answer that might be more valid," his father explained.

"Are you all geniuses?" Liv asked.

"By scientific definition, a genius is a person with an IQ of at least one hundred and sixty," his mother explained

"Is that high?" Liv asked.

"Average IQ is considered to be between ninety and one hundred and ten, and approximately fifty percent of the population is contained in that range."

"And how many people are above one-sixty?" I asked.

"Approximately one in every thirty-three hundred people," his mother answered.

"So that means there are potentially five geniuses in our town," I said.

"Yeah, right," Liv said.

"I'm just going by the odds."

"And I'm going by all the people I know," Liv said. "Have you seen much genius at work around here?"

"But most experts in the field of human learning and intelligence would argue that a definition of genius cannot be based on something as basic and derivative as an IQ number," his mother continued.

"Perhaps any person who ascribes to the numerical definition of genius automatically *disqualifies* themselves from the category of genius," his father said.

The two of them and Gene started laughing. Apparently, this was their idea of a joke. Did they even joke on a smarter level?

"What would Einstein's IQ have been?" Liv asked.

"Well above one-sixty, but he demonstrated so much more that would be considered true genius. He was able to apply abstract reasoning, non-parallel thinking, creative problem solving, and the ability to synthesize and amalgamate information to form new concepts and ideas."

Liv turned to me. "Did you understand any of that?"

"A bit."

"So, back to my question, are you three geniuses?"

Nobody answered.

"Don't be humble. Do you all have IQs above one-sixty?"

Gene looked to his parents, and they both nodded like they were giving him permission to answer.

"We all would satisfy that numeric assessment. Will I take those SAT tests?" Gene asked.

"If you want to get in to university," Liv said. "Do you want to study with us sometime?"

"Yes. Should we start tonight?"

"I think we're through for the day," I said.

"All that's left is ice cream," Liv said. "So, are you going to join us?"

"We gave permission, as it does seem like an appropriate teen-aged activity," his mother said.

"I concur," his father added.

"One thing first," Liv said. "Gene, you might want to rethink your wardrobe."

Gene looked down at his shirt and shorts. "What should I put on?"

"Anything else except your blue suit," Liv replied.

He disappeared out of the room, and I heard him going up the stairs. I turned back around, and his parents were staring at me again.

"Um, thanks for inviting us in," I stammered.

"And you are welcome — both of you — to visit with us again."

8

WE WERE HEADING to the ice cream parlor downtown because they had the biggest cones in town. Their double cones were bigger than anybody else's triple, and their triple was so big that it took two hands to hold. I almost started to drool thinking about it.

Gene was in shiny leather shoes, dress pants held up by suspenders, and a button-down collared shirt that was tucked in to his pants. We were headed to get ice cream, and he was dressed for a job interview — two decades ago.

"Are you going to explain those shorts you were wearing?" Liv asked.

"I was going out to rehearse my shooting skills," Gene said. "I do not own any shorts, so I made them."

"That still doesn't explain why you cut them so short," Liv exclaimed.

"They were the right length. I measured before I cut."

"Then you measured wrong," she said.

"I would never do that. I looked at pictures of Michael Jordan, and knowing his height I was able to calculate the exact length the shorts needed to be on me."

"Those were how they wore basketball shorts in 1993," I explained.

"That's when he and his team completed the three-peat, winning the NBA championship for the third time. They defeated the Phoenix Suns, led by Charles Barkley. Jordan averaged forty-one points per game and was named the finals' MVP for a third straight year, a feat previously reached only by Earvin Johnson, who is also known as Magic Johnson."

"Look, if you're going to be talking old school you should at least be talking about Indiana's own Larry Bird," Liv suggested.

"Larry Bird played for Indiana State University, leading them to the finals in which they lost to Michigan State, led by the previously mentioned Earvin 'Magic' Johnson. He then was drafted by the Boston Celtics and played from 1979 until —"

"Yeah, yeah, thanks for the history of basketball lesson," Liv said.

Was this the same guy who couldn't name any other player except Michael Jordan just a few days ago? Had he been studying basketball?

"You have to take those shorts and burn them," Liv said.

Gene looked at me for my opinion.

"She's right. Not about the burning part, but you should toss them out."

Then I started thinking. Cutting down a pair of pants to make shorts, researching basketball, and, of course, going out to "rehearse shooting" on the driveway. He didn't even know to call it "practice," but there was no question that he was going to try out for the team.

"You definitely need new basketball shorts," I suggested.

"Let's be honest, you basically need an entire new wardrobe," Liv added.

"Liv!"

"Sometimes you have to be cruel to be kind." She turned to Gene. "Have you noticed that you dress differently from everybody at school?"

"Mr. McCarthy dresses like me."

"He's a seventy-year-old English teacher and not the role model you should be aiming for," Liv said.

"Becky, would you help me pick out new clothes?"

"I think it might even be part of my job in helping you fit in."

We came to the town square. There were lots of people, and, of course, we knew everybody.

The line for the ice cream parlor was out the door and snaking its way along the whole front of the store. It looked like there were two girls' soccer teams — green uniforms for one team and red for the other — along with assorted parents.

"How badly do you want ice cream?" Liv asked me.

"Not that much. Gene, are you okay with not getting ice cream tonight?"

"Do you think we could do something else instead?" Gene asked.

"What did you have in mind?"

He pointed across the square. "Could we go shopping for clothes?"

"Right now?" Liv asked.

"It is open, and I would like to. You both think I need them."

I turned to Liv. "We could get him a few things. A pair of jeans, a couple of T-shirts, maybe some basketball shoes."

"And some basketball shorts," she added.

"Do you have any money on you, or a credit card?" I asked.

Gene reached into his pocket and pulled out a thick wad of cash. I was shocked by the size of it.

"Would this be enough?"

"How much do you have?"

"Eight hundred dollars."

Liv and I looked at each other.

"Most people don't walk around with that much cash on them," I said.

"My parents believe in making only cash transactions."

"I thought that only drug dealers did everything in cash," Liv said and laughed.

I laughed along — sort of in support. Gene just looked confused.

"She doesn't think your parents are drug dealers," I explained.

"Let's do it!" Liv exclaimed.

GENE WAS NOW dressed in faded jeans, a white T-shirt, and new basketball shoes. The shoes, Air Jordans, were actually the identical bright blue of his suit. In a suit it was bad, on the shoes it was good. Liv had already told him that he was forbidden to wear these shoes and that suit together.

What had started as an item or two had taken up most of Gene's cash. I'd asked him if his parents would be okay with this, and he said he knew they would. I wasn't so sure. He'd asked if he could come and get an ice cream and instead was coming home with a full new wardrobe.

Gene seemed to be almost bouncing in his new Jordans. It was more than a spring and less than a skip. He had a big grin on his face. It made me smile too. He had an infectious sort of happiness to him.

A siren sounded right behind us, and I jumped. There was a police car on the road right behind us slowly rolling along. Of course, I knew who it was.

"Put your hands in the air!" came a voice over the loudspeaker.

Gene dropped his bags to the ground and raised his hands.

"You don't have to do that," I said. "It's Liv's father."

The car stopped, and Liv's father got out. Liv put down the bags she was carrying and gave her father a hug.

"Did you three rip off a store?" her father asked.

"No, sir, we have the receipts," Gene said.

"Gene, he's joking, it's just a joke."

"I don't blame Gene for being confused," Liv said. "That was a classic dad joke, so it wasn't really funny at all."

"This must be Gene," her father said.

"Yes, sir."

"I'm Liv's father, Kevin Riley. And you can call me Officer Riley."

"Yes, sir," Gene said as they shook hands.

"He's joking," Liv said.

"That depends. Are you dating my daughter?"

"Dad!"

"No, sir."

"Then you can call me Kevin, but if you ever do start dating my daughter, I have a gun and I know how to use it."

Gene turned to Liv. "A joke, right?"

"Possibly. And isn't it now obvious why I'm not asked out more often?" Liv asked.

"Just out of curiosity, have you ever pulled your gun in this town?" I asked.

"Here? Come on, get real. It looks like you kids were on a real shopping spree."

"We took Gene to get new clothes," I said.

"Probably wise not to go wandering about in a bright blue suit," Liv's father said.

"You know about Gene's suit?" I asked.

"Becky, in a town this big everybody knows about everybody's suit."

"*Everybody* knows about everybody's *everything*," Liv added.

"Although I didn't stop to talk about clothes," Liv's father said. "Raise your hand if you forgot you had to babysit your cousin this evening."

"Oh, my goodness! It slipped my mind!" Liv exclaimed.

"Your aunt sent me out to find you. She said she and your uncle haven't been on a real date in almost two years, and she wasn't letting anything get in the way. You better climb on in."

"Sorry, Gene, sorry Becky."

She gave me a hug and then hugged Gene. He didn't pull away, but he didn't hug her back.

They climbed into the car and drove away, and the siren and lights came on. This was as close to an emergency as ever seemed to happen around here. We reshuffled the bags with Gene taking most of them.

"I have a question," I said. "Why is your last name different from your parents?"

"My mother kept her name."

"Then shouldn't you be Gene Lawrence or Gene Wilson and not Gene Newman?"

"I am adopted. Newman is my original name."

"Oh, I didn't know. I didn't mean to get personal."

"Could I ask *you* a question?" he asked.

"Sure."

"How long have you been getting headaches?"

"Did somebody mention that to you?"

He shook his head. "You had one the day we met. Today was not originally as bad but has become more intense over the past hour. You were just rubbing your temples, and your shoulders are now more tense and slightly elevated."

"I'm just surprised that you noticed that."

"I notice everything," he said.

I couldn't stop myself from laughing — and then felt bad and stopped.

"I notice, but that does not mean I understand or can put things into the proper context. Humor is probably the most difficult for me to understand."

"Really, I hadn't noticed," I said.

"Ah, sarcasm. Sarcasm is the lowest form of wit but the highest form of intelligence."

"What?"

"A quote from Oscar Wilde. He was an Irish playwright, essayist, and humorist born in 1854 who died in 1900."

"It almost sounds like you've been researching humor."

"How else would I learn about it?"

That actually made sense in a Gene sort of way.

"Are you going to answer my question?" he asked.

"Question? Oh, about the headaches. I've had them for the past couple of years. They come and they go, but they've been worse the last few months."

"Do you worry about it being a brain tumor?"

"Of course not!"

"Really, never?" he asked.

"Well ... sometimes, I guess."

"It is not a tumor," Gene said.

"It's nice of you to say that."

"I was not trying to be nice. It's simple knowledge."

"Are you an expert on brains as well as humor?" I asked.

"Nice joke," he said and smiled. He had such a great smile. "I have done additional reading about human physiology and neurological functioning. If it was a tumor, it would be getting significantly worse and would be more constant instead of coming and going."

"That's what the doctor said."

"And if it was a tumor, it would have shown on your MRIs, and they were clear."

"Yes, but ... wait, how did you know that I had MRIs?"

How could he know that? Had Liv told him?

"That would be standard medical investigation when somebody is having recurring headaches with no other causal factor."

"But you said MRIs, plural."

"You would need to have a series of MRIs to not only fully rule out a tumor but to see if there were any changes in brain structure or brain activity."

"That's what my doctor said as well."

"By eliminating a physical cause, they are thereby assigning the causation of your headaches to a psychological reason."

"They say that I worry too much."

"You do worry too much," Gene said. "You carry your stress in your upper body."

"What?"

"You tense up. I can see your shoulders rise up and your neck becomes stiff and you turn your body to compensate for not wanting to turn your head. It has even gotten more noticeable since we started this discussion."

He was right. Maybe he did notice everything.

"Put down the bags," he said. I hesitated. "Put them down."

I set the bags down on the sidewalk, and he did the same with his. Gene moved in behind me, and I was shocked when he placed his hands on my shoulders. "This is the focal point of the tension."

He placed his fingers on the front of my shoulders and dug his thumbs into the blades on both sides. It hurt slightly. Then the pain gave way to ache, and then I could feel the stress leaving. I let out a little groan.

"Am I hurting you?"

"No, not really. It feels good."

My shoulders began slowly falling like balloons with a leak releasing the air. I let out another groan. I could feel the pressure in my head ease off too.

"Does that feel better?"

"Much better."

He continued to knead my shoulders. "There are pressure points here and here," he said, digging in his thumbs.

I could feel the headache easing even more.

"The mind and body are connected. The pain is caused by physiological factors, even if those have their cause in psychological reasons. You need to be treated by a massage therapist on a regular basis. I assume there is one in town."

"I guess there is."

"You should think about it."

I groaned a little in response. "Let me guess, you read a book about massage and pressure points to relieve stress."

"I have a general knowledge of anatomy, and I read two specific articles yesterday."

"Why would you read those articles?"

"I thought it would be good information for me to know."

I turned to face him. "Was it because you saw I was having headaches?"

He looked embarrassed as he nodded. "Is this like me switching to music? Should I have asked your permission before I did the research?"

"No, you don't need to ask me about what you read! It's just, well, it's strange to have somebody doing that — you know, reading up on things."

"I am sorry."

"You don't have to be sorry. I guess I should say thank you for helping me. For thinking about me." I paused. "Not many people do."

I turned away and picked up the bags and started walking. He fell in beside me.

"They should," he said.

"They should what?"

"Think about you. You are smart. You are a good person. You are helping me."

"Thanks."

Would he still think that if he knew I was only helping him because I'd been asked to and I thought it would look good on my university applications?

"I'm glad I can help you," I said instead.

"And I could help you, too," he said. "Not just with the headache. My parents are right; I could help you study for the SATs or for tests." He paused. "If you want me to."

"I'd like that."

"Good. And thank you for helping me select clothes."

"You look nice … I mean, the clothes look nice. It was fun. It was sort of like dressing a big life-sized Barbie, or I guess Ken."

"Barbie and Ken? Do they go to our school?"

I couldn't stop myself from laughing and then felt bad for doing it. Once again Gene looked embarrassed.

"Barbie is a doll, and Ken is her boyfriend doll. I guess you never had a Barbie. Did you have a G.I. Joe?"

He shook his head. "Is that another doll? I could do some research to —"

"You don't have to research Barbie dolls. Gene, you are one strange combination of things you know and things you don't know," I said. "Not that it's your fault."

"I am going to work harder to fit in and be like everybody else."

"There's nothing wrong with being different. You really are unique. You're one of a kind."

Gene smiled. "You have no idea how right you are."

9

I PUSHED MRS. PHILLIPS' chair along the hall of the nursing home. Lunch was finished, and I was helping the nurses and aides get everybody out of the dining hall and back to their rooms.

My phone rang. Still pushing with one hand, I pulled it out to answer. I didn't recognize the number, silenced it, and put it back in my pocket.

"Here we go, Mrs. Phillips," I said. I wheeled her into her room and over to her favorite chair.

"Thank you, Rebecca."

Everybody here called me by my real name. I'd filled out the volunteer forms that way, and even my mother called me Rebecca when I was working. At first it had sounded strange, but I was starting to think I was too old to go by Becky. Becky was a seven-year-old and not a seventeen-year-old. Maybe next year, when I started university, I'd start going exclusively by Rebecca.

I locked the wheels on the chair, clicked back the footrests, and took a half step back. Mrs. Phillips was old and frail, but she was also proud and independent. It was a balance between being close enough to help if needed, but far enough away not to make it look that way. She braced herself and slowly got up from the wheelchair and eased herself into her favorite chair beside the bed.

"Thank you so much, dear."

My phone rang again.

"It's all right if you want to get that," she said.

I looked at the phone. It was that same number. "I don't know the number, so it's probably somebody just trying to sell me something."

"Only one way to find out."

I answered. "Hello."

"Hello, Becky."

"Gene?"

"Yes. I hoped it would be all right for me to call."

"No, of course it is. I just can't talk much because I'm at the nursing home doing my volunteer work."

"I know. You always work on Sunday mornings. I wanted to try out my new phone."

"A new phone is always so exciting!"

"This is my first phone."

"You never had a phone before?"

"I never needed one before."

"I know you were homeschooled, but how did you talk to your friends?"

As soon as I said it, I felt bad. Did he have any friends? Is that why he seemed so desperate to talk to me? Then I thought, did somebody have to be desperate to want to talk to me?

"Congrats on the new phone. Show it to me at school tomorrow."

"I will not be in attendance tomorrow and possibly Tuesday," Gene said.

"Are you sick?"

"I have to work with my parents on some potential changes in their research."

"You help them with their research?"

"Sometimes. I will see you in biology on Wednesday."

"Do you want me to take notes for you?" I asked.

"Notes?"

"On what's being taught so that you won't ..." I suddenly realized how ridiculous my offer was. He didn't need to read notes, or even attend class, to do well. "And thank you for calling."

"Really?"

"I would have wondered about you, worried you were sick if you weren't in school."

"I try not to worry you, and, Becky, thank you for being my friend."

"Sure, no problem." That sounded so lame. "See you on Wednesday."

I hung up. "Sorry," I said to Mrs. Phillips.

"Your boyfriend should always have priority over an old woman."

"You're not an old woman, well, not that old, you know, compared to some of the people here, and he isn't my boyfriend."

"It sounded like he was your boyfriend."

"He's just a friend. I don't even have a boyfriend!"

"A pretty girl like you, kind, smart. Why don't you have a boyfriend?"

"I don't have time."

"But you have time to volunteer to work here?"

"That's part of the reason I don't have time."

"Tell me about your *friend*."

"I'm not sure what I can tell you."

"Tell me anything."

I shrugged. "Well, like you heard me say on the phone, his name is Gene, and he's new to town. He and his parents just moved here from New York."

"New York is such a wonderful city. My Tommy and I, rest his soul, had our honeymoon there."

She gestured to one of the pictures of her late husband that dominated a whole wall of her bedroom. He was very handsome.

"He's actually from a little town in New York State. It's near a place called Plattsburgh."

"Is he a nice boy?"

"He's very nice. Thoughtful."

"Thoughtful is not so common. Is he smart?" Mrs. Phillips asked.

"He's probably the smartest person I've ever met — well, except for maybe his parents."

"You met his parents?"

"At his house, he invited us in. But really, it was my friend Liv's idea that we sort of dropped by his house."

"Is he good-looking like my Tommy?" she asked, gesturing back to the pictures again.

I thought about that blue suit and the strange hair and the stranger behavior, but really. "He is. He's tall, and he has a nice smile."

"Is he built?"

"Mrs. Phillips!"

"Look, Rebecca. I'm old, I'm not dead. Is he, what do you kids say, is he hot?"

"I think that was actually the word Liv used to describe him."

"It sounds like your friend might be interested, even if you're not."

"She's not, really."

Mrs. Phillips gave me a look like she didn't believe me. "Is this Gene kind to you? Does he treat you well, does he do nice things for you?"

I didn't even have to think to answer. "Yes, he's very nice to me. He's considerate and kind and there's a gentleness to him."

"So, he's smart, nice, good-looking, gentle, and treats you well and you're not interested in him. Is that right?"

"I didn't say that."

"Then you *are* interested?" she asked.

"I haven't known him that long."

"I only knew my Tommy for three days when I knew that he was the one. Besides, I'm not saying you should get married, just that you go have some fun. What would be the harm?"

What would be the harm?

"Love is a funny thing. It can happen fast or it can happen slow, or even slowly and then all at once."

I didn't really understand what she meant.

"But when it happens, you'll know it," she said. "Nobody will have to explain it."

Would I know being in love the way she knew it for her Tommy, or the way my parents knew it?

She let out a big sigh. "Do you remember being ten years old?"

"Yeah, sure, of course."

"I remember being ten and eighteen and thirty-seven and sixty-five and eighty. It passes like that," she said and snapped her fingers. "Sometimes I look into a mirror and wonder who's that old woman staring back at me?" She paused. "Do you know what I'm saying?"

"That time flies."

"Flies so fast. You can't waste it, and you can't wait. What are you waiting for?"

I shrugged. "Maybe he isn't interested in me."

"What do you think that phone call was about? Besides, why wouldn't he be interested in you? You're all those things you said he was, smart, nice, kind, and good-looking. Although a little more makeup would be good, and you could wear things that are a little more revealing. If I still had it, you think I wouldn't show it?"

I laughed and felt myself start to blush.

"I won't even see him until Wednesday."

"You could call. Aren't you almost finished for today?"

I looked at my watch. "In about fifteen minutes."

"Go a little early. Make a call."

I nodded in agreement. "I'll see you next week."

She reached out and gave my hand a little squeeze. "I'll be waiting for a full report. Will you tell me what happened?"

"Of course." I paused. "That is, if you promise not to tell my mother what I tell you."

"Promise."

I bent down and gave her a hug around the neck. I left the room, phone in hand, and almost bumped in to Mrs. Edleman, the home administrator. She gave me a stern look. She actually scared me.

"No need for speed, Rebecca," she said. "Slow and steady."

"Yes, ma'am." I hoped she hadn't noticed my phone.

"Rebecca, we're short-staffed. Would it be possible for you to stay an extra hour to settle some more of our residents into their rooms?"

"Yes, of course."

She nodded. "You are very mature, very conscientious in your work. Thank you."

She hurried off. So much for leaving early. So much for calling Gene. I slipped the phone back into my pocket. I could call him later tonight, or even tomorrow. Or just wait until I saw him on Wednesday.

10

THE GIRLS WERE already at the table eating as I crossed the cafeteria. I was late because Ms. Freeman had kept me after class asking about Gene and when was he going to be back after missing Monday and Tuesday's classes. I told her I was pretty sure he'd be back tomorrow, which made her happy. Apparently, she planned to have him to play a solo at the next school assembly and wanted to make sure he had time to prepare. I had the feeling that he could have shown up five minutes before the assembly and played any piece he was given sight unseen and still gotten it perfect. He kept showing how amazing he was on the sax.

I set down my tray, said hellos, and took a seat. The conversation that was already going on was a variation on the same ones we'd had all the time for the past three years. Maybe it was true that not much new happened in this town, but it was also true that not much new happened at this table.

I was startled as Liv snapped her fingers right in front of my eyes. "Are you in there?"

I gave her a confused look.

"We were talking to you, and it was like you didn't hear us," Sasha added.

"Another headache?" Emma asked.

"No, I haven't had one of those since, well, since Saturday."
I almost said since Gene gave me a massage, but that would have
sounded bad, or wrong, or at least misleading.

"Not at all?" Liv asked.

"Not really — you know, a little pressure, but not the same."

"That's so good. Does that mean you don't need to go for any
more tests?" Liv asked.

"I've got another scan scheduled in —" My phone vibrated in
my pocket. "I have a call."

It was Gene.

"Hello. How are you doing?" I asked.

"Very fine. And you?"

"Who is it?" Liv asked.

I put the phone aside. "Gene," I whispered.

"Tell him we miss him!" Emma said.

"Maybe you should tell him yourself." I pushed the speaker
button and put the phone down on the table. "You're on speaker,
Gene."

"We miss you!" Sasha called out.

"I miss all of you. Becky, could I join you for lunch?"

"You know you always can," I said, and the others agreed.

"So, you're going to be back tomorrow?" I asked.

"I am back today. I am at the cash register."

I looked over. He was standing there holding a tray, his pack
slung over one shoulder, and he waved at us.

"You're in your new clothes!" Liv said.

"And your hair is different, isn't it?" Emma asked.

"I got it cut and styled."

"Come and join us," I said and hung up.

Gene moved across the cafeteria. New shirt, faded jeans, and his Jordans. His hair was not just different but very nice. On his tray was a heaping double serving of French fries.

"Your clothes are different, and your hair looks fantastic!" Sasha said.

"Thank you." He looked happy but hesitant. "Becky, do you like it? Does my hair look fantastic?"

I laughed. "I don't know about fantastic, but it does look good."

He smiled, and that made me smile.

"It was styled by the barber in the town square," Gene explained. "He asked me how I wanted it cut, and I pointed at a picture on the wall."

"You pointed at the right picture," Emma said. "You look really good."

Was Emma interested in Gene as well?

"Why did you call instead of just coming over?" I asked.

"I like using my phone. It is pretty cool, right?" He held up his new iPhone. It was the same as my phone, right down to the same protective case.

"Let me put in my number," Liv said as she took it from him and punched her digits in.

I felt a pang of jealousy. "Put in Emma's and Sasha's numbers as well," I said. "I already know you have *my* number." I just had to throw that in.

I'd thought about calling Gene a dozen times over the last couple of days. I'd even gone as far as pulling out my phone and stopped myself. Maybe I should have called him.

"I thought you weren't going to be back until tomorrow," I said.

"I wanted to get back sooner, so we worked harder."

"He was doing some work with his parents," I explained to the others.

"They're scientists, right?" Emma asked.

"Yes, they're both research scientists," I said, answering for him.

"What are they researching?" Sasha asked.

"My parents are investigating the interface between human physiology and brain functioning."

"What?" Liv asked.

"They are studying the limits of human intelligence."

"You make it sound like they're studying *your* brain," Liv said and laughed.

Emma and Sasha joined in. Gene didn't. He just looked uncomfortable. I wanted to give him a way out.

"That's a lot of French fries," I said, pointing down at his tray.

"Yes, they are really good!" he said and then popped two into his mouth.

"I think the cheeseburger is great," Emma said. "You should try that as well."

"The cheeseburger is meat, and he's a vegetarian, remember?" I asked.

"I forgot. Still, my guess is that there isn't any real meat in burgers they serve here," Emma joked.

"I respect Gene for what he's doing," I said.

He looked happy. Very happy. He opened his backpack and started to pull out the things we'd seen at other lunches — bags of vegetables, fruit, and very healthy-looking sandwiches. He started digging in, and the conversation went back to the usual topics.

"What are those?" Liv asked, pointing at his backpack.

Before he could answer, she reached inside his backpack and pulled out some magazines. She spread them across the table. There were a couple of *People*, an *Us Weekly*, and a few copies of *Vogue*.

"You read *Vogue*?" Emma asked.

"What's wrong with *Vogue*?" I asked. "I read *Vogue*."

"No, you don't," Liv said.

"I read it when I'm standing in line at the supermarket with my mother. There's nothing wrong with reading things like that."

"I love *People* magazine," Emma said. "How else can I find out what's really happening in the world?"

I figured he was reading them as research on how to fit in. Again, time to change the subject. "Mr. Benjamin said we have a test on Friday. Do you want to get together to study?"

"Yes. Would you want to come to my home?" Gene asked.

"Sure. How about tonight after dinner?"

"Would six-thirty be good?" he asked.

"Perfect. We have a date … you know … a study date."

11

"I'LL BE UP in a minute," Gene said. "I need to talk to my parents. You know the way, correct?"

I was happy to leave his parents behind. They'd asked me lots and lots of questions, and not the normal sort of questions. It felt more like a job interview or a medical examination, or like I was part of a science project. I almost expected them to pull out clipboards and start ticking off boxes as I answered.

Even more specifically, they'd asked a lot of questions about my headaches. They'd even asked about my MRIs. Obviously, Gene had mentioned all of this to them. Maybe he'd even asked them for advice. After all, they were brain scientists. I guessed they were interested in that sort of stuff. They seemed as socially awkward as their son. He might have been adopted, but it seemed to be a case of nurture over nature.

As I hit the final flight of stairs, I couldn't help thinking about the hundreds of times I'd been up here. Sarah had deliberately chosen this room, up on its own floor, separate from her parents' bedroom, which was on the second level. I would have been afraid to be that far away from my parents when I was little. Sarah wasn't afraid of much.

I stopped at the closed bedroom door. It was painted pink, and in the center of the door there was a small rectangular patch that was a deeper shade of pink. That patch used to be covered by a name tag that had identified this as "Sarah's World." I hadn't even thought about that plaque until I saw the patch.

I turned the knob, opened the door, and stepped in. It was like stepping back in time.

On the far wall was Sarah's bed with the big brass headboard. Draped on the corner of the headboard was a large, fancy-looking set of headphones beside a second smaller set, and on the night table was an expensive-looking sound system. He didn't seem like the type to listen to music at all, but I wouldn't have been surprised if he'd memorized all of the top songs so he could fit in.

The bed was neatly made, and folded up at the bottom was a mauve bedspread with little red flowers that were arranged in a geometric pattern. It was Sarah's. It was just as I remembered from my last time here.

There was one big change, though. Against the far wall was a gigantic metal desk. Atop it was a computer with a monitor that stretched the length of the desk. On the back corner was a really expensive-looking 3D printer. I'd never seen one that big before.

There was also a stack of books on top of the scanner. I walked over and recognized the top book — it was the SAT preparation guide I was using. Was Gene studying to take the SATs? I lifted it up, and right beneath was our biology textbook. I picked it up as well. Underneath it was our calculus text, and below that our history text, followed by a book about advanced saxophone techniques and the complete Grover Washington Jr. songbook.

Then at the very bottom were three books about basketball — coaching techniques, strategies, and basic plays. Did he really think he could read his way on to a basketball team? I put the books back down, trying to pile them in the same order. I didn't want him to know I'd been snooping.

Beside the textbooks was a pile of blank white paper. Wait, the paper wasn't blank; there was something on the page, but it wasn't in ink. I picked up the top sheet. It had ridges and bumps. I turned it to the side to look at it more closely and then ran my finger along it. This was braille. Why would Gene have braille? Was he learning to read it like somebody else would learn a second language?

I heard somebody coming up the steps, and I quickly put down the sheet on top of the pile and then rushed over to the window, getting there just before Gene entered the room.

"Sorry for taking so long," Gene said.

"No problem. I was just here, looking out the window. There's a beautiful breeze blowing in."

He walked over to my side. "You used to climb that tree."

"All the time and all the way to the top."

The one big branch was so close that it was almost in the room. I reached out and put my hand on it.

"Are you thinking of leafing?" he asked.

"I'm not leaving."

"I said *leafing*. It is a tree, and it has leaves."

"That is a terrible joke."

"I am making a pun, which is a joke that utilizes words that sound alike but have different meanings."

"Okay, then it's a terrible pun. Oh, that's right, you've been studying humor." I wanted to ask if he'd also been studying basketball, but that would have let him know I'd been looking through his stuff.

"Humor is a difficult subject to examine from an academic perspective. Some things seem to have less to do with the head and more to do with the soul."

"That's how I feel about this tree," I said. "I miss this tree."

"The way you miss your friend Sarah?"

I nodded. "It feels like if I turned around quickly, I'd see her standing there. If I opened the closet, her clothes would be hanging there."

"Not her clothes, but there were some things left that I assumed were hers," he said. "I will show you."

He opened the closet door. Hanging there instead of Sarah's clothing was his — two or three suits, including the blue one, some shirts, including the new ones we'd purchased, and some sweaters.

"Was this hers?" Gene asked as he pulled out a field hockey stick.

"Yes, it's sort of sad," I said.

"Sad?"

"Have you ever had a good friend move away?"

"I have never had a good friend." He paused. "I have never had any friends."

"Never?"

"I did not go to school. I lived in a compound. I never played in a band or was on a sports team."

"That was insensitive of me."

"Insensitive?"

"I didn't mean to say anything that would hurt your feelings."

"It is not like you were saying anything that I did not know.

I have never really had a friend before, so sometimes I say things that are inappropriate or strange or just plain wrong."

I was going to argue, but he was right, and we both knew it.

"But I think I know intellectually what it would be like. I did lose my parents — my real parents."

"Do you ever wonder what your biological parents were like?"

"I read their profiles."

"I don't know what that means," I said.

"There is a file that has information about who they are, and I have full access. They were young, university aged. They were healthy. My hair texture and color are similar to my mother's, and both my parents had blue eyes, as do I. My father was athletic, and they both had IQs in the one-thirty-five range, which is in the very superior category."

"I guess you come by your smarts naturally."

"Naturally is not the word I would associate with it."

What did that mean? "Does it say why they gave you up?"

He didn't answer but looked even more uncomfortable. The silence went on for a while before he spoke.

"I am aware of the reasons."

Another pause followed. I hated awkward silence.

"My natural mother now lives in Florida, and my natural father recently moved to Canada."

"That's in the profile?"

He shook his head. "I am able to track them through the internet." He paused. "Nobody knows that I do that."

"I'd do the same thing."

"You would?"

"It's normal to want to know."

"Most of the time I am not sure what normal is." Once again, he paused. He looked sad. "That has been the hardest part. So much you know as normal I am discovering for the first time. Sometimes it all seems so much that I find myself overwhelmed. I need time alone to try to process."

"Like a computer."

"Like a human. Fitting in is so hard."

"I understand."

Then I thought of something I wanted to tell him and hadn't been brave enough. "If you wanted to fit in a little bit better, you could change the way you talk."

"I do not understand."

"You *don't* understand," I said.

"Yes, I do not understand," he repeated.

"You need to start using contractions. Don't say *do not*, say *don't*. Not *I am*, but *I'm*. Normally, people talk in contractions."

"I did not … I mean I didn't really notice. I will … I'll try."

"Good. And by the way, that's quite a setup you have," I said, pointing at his desk. "Is that a 3D printer?"

"Yes. I use it to convert written text to braille."

"You're learning to read braille?"

"*I've* read using braille as early as I could read using my eyes."

I smiled. "Good use of contractions. So, it's sort of like speaking another language."

"It's another format to input information."

"Once again, that makes it sound like you're a computer."

"We *all* are, but such a different type of computer. Let me explain. Please have a seat." He pulled out the desk chair, and I sat.

"There are things that it would be best if you kept in confidence."

"Then maybe you shouldn't tell me," I said.

"Most is public domain, common knowledge to neurologists, scientists, and researchers, things that my parents or others have already published."

"But you still don't want me to talk to anybody around here about it," I said.

"It would be better if you did not — *didn't* — discuss it with your parents or even Liv."

"Then I won't. I promise, but I have a question for you ... well, *about* you." I paused before going further. "Are you part of your parents' research?"

He smiled. "I told them that you'd come to that conclusion. I am a *part* of the research. They're studying ways to create and enhance human intelligence and to increase learning strategies."

"Obviously successful techniques. Look at you. So, you can teach me things that would make me as smart as you?"

He shook his head. "That's not possible." He stopped. "I didn't mean to offend you."

"No offense. I get it. I don't know anybody who's as smart as you, except maybe your parents. Wait, are your parents as smart as you?"

He didn't answer, but he looked uncertain if he should.

"I'm different from them. I really can help you produce enhanced results. Your marks will improve. I could do that if you wanted me to."

"I do. Let's put on some music and get started." I pointed to his sound system.

"It's not used for music. Music is not only ineffective but counterproductive to successful studying."

"But I always have music on when I study."

"And that would be at least partially why your studying hasn't had optimal success. When you study while listening to music, the information is stored in a part of your brain that's only fully accessible for retrieval when similar stimulus is applied."

"What?"

"Have you ever had the experience that information is right there, but you can't quite retrieve it?"

"All the time. It's on the tip of my tongue."

"In those situations, you have the information stored, but you cannot retrieve it. Neurons that wire together, fire together."

"We're back to me being confused." I was starting to wonder if I wasn't smart enough to become smarter.

"Are you able to listen to music when you're taking tests?"

"Of course not," I said.

"And that explains why you have difficulty retrieving it. There is an association between the manner in which information is stored — neurons being wired — and then retrieved — neurons fired. Put simply, the same paired stimuli, the music, is necessary to retrieve information."

"I guess I understand."

"Retrieval is the key. Test results are *not* based on what information you possess but what you're able to demonstrate knowledge of. Listening to music while studying blocks your ability to retrieve information. In fact, all multitasking works that way."

"But we're always multitasking. They tell us in school how important it is for us to learn to multitask."

"Every scientific study ever done has shown that multitasking compromises task functioning. What is effective instead of multi-*tasking* is to utilize multi*sensory* input."

"Again, not making any sensory sense."

"You have five senses. The brain is open to accepting input through all five of those senses."

"Sure, of course."

"But each sense contributes different quantities of raw information. Which sense do you think contributes the most information?"

"Sight probably, followed by sound."

"Exactly right. Visual input accounts for eighty-three percent of our information input, followed by auditory at around eleven percent. Those two senses provide ninety-four percent of input."

"And only six percent comes through the other three senses," I said.

"Smell is around three and a half percent, touch about one and a half percent, and taste about one percent."

"I guess that sounds right."

"Of course, there are exceptions. A rock climber uses touch and associated qualities like balance to get continual input from their skin and muscles and tendons vis-à-vis their place on the cliff face. A chef uses taste more extensively than anybody else would ever utilize that sense."

"But what about people who are deaf or blind? Are you saying they lose all of that, that they can't learn as much because they lack that sense?"

"No. The brain is flexible. It learns to fully adapt and expands those sensory inputs that are available. The brain makes additional space for those multisensory inputs that are providing information."

"I don't understand."

"Deaf people have a greater sense of peripheral vision. Those who are blind have a more acute sense of hearing. Those parts of the brain that are not receiving information are absorbed by other senses, allowing a greater level of input and processing from those senses. Real estate in the brain is far too valuable to be left vacant."

"And you read braille to build something in that spot," I said.

He nodded his head. "I get information not only through my ears and eyes but through my sense of touch. When I'm learning something new, I don't just read it, I hear it, and I feel it through my fingertips."

I realized he was not talking exclusively without contractions. He'd already adapted and used my suggestion.

"Does that make sense?" he asked.

"Sure. So that braille on your desk is the braille version of the textbooks?"

He smiled. "I didn't know you'd noticed them, but exactly."

"But it's not like I can learn to read braille," I said.

"You *could* learn, but that isn't a feasible adjunct learning modality for you. You wouldn't be able to input at a rate that would allow it to be in sync with the visual and auditory tracking fields."

"So, hearing and seeing."

"Exactly."

"Then how are you going to help me learn more, or better, or whatever you're going to do?" I asked.

"We're going to combine some of the techniques I use. Come to my bed. I want you to put on these headphones."

"Sure, but why do you have two sets of headphones?"

"The smaller ones aren't headphones. They're neurological stimulators. They administer an electrical pulse through my brain."

I think my expression betrayed what I was thinking.

"Research has shown that passing a mild electrical current through the neural tissue supports the formation of connected neural pathways, which then facilitates both learning and retrieval."

I shook my head. "I don't think I want to do that."

"I'm not suggesting that you utilize that technique."

"Oh, okay, good."

I sat down on the edge of the bed.

"In anticipation of you agreeing, I've preloaded the audio unit with the next three chapters in our biology unit."

"I've already read those chapters. I've started studying for the test."

"And if you were listening to music then you inputted the information in a way that it can't be fully retrieved." He handed me the book. "What you need to do is read the chapters while the same words are read out loud to you."

"So, I'll hear them and see them at the same time. Multi-sensory, is that the right word?"

"In this case it's bi-sensory because it involves two senses. You need to coordinate the pace of your reading with the speed of the auditory representation. They have to be completely in sync."

He went to hand me the headphones, and his hand brushed against my neck. The fingers of his hand stroked the side of my neck and then moved onto my shoulders. That wasn't an accident. He ran his hand along my neck and —

"I'm so pleased to see that your tension level is low," he said.

That's what he was doing. He was assessing my stress level and nothing else. I was relieved and, I had to admit, a little bit disappointed and felt awkward. I had to say something.

"And I'm pleased to hear you using contractions."

"I adapt quickly to new stimuli and situations. The controls are here on the player. You can adjust the speed with this knob. I'll leave you and be back in sixty minutes."

"You're not going to stay?"

"My presence would interfere with your input. I also have some independent study I need to complete."

Gene left the room, closing the door behind him.

I went to put on the headphones and realized that I needed to text my parents that I was going to be here for a while. I pulled out my phone and noticed there was only one flickering bar of reception. I walked over to the window and got two more. I texted that I wouldn't be home for at least two hours and that we were studying. I went to put the phone away and then stopped. I turned it right off. No distractions.

And then I heard something through the open window. I recognized it immediately — a basketball bouncing against pavement. That could mean only one thing. Gene's independent research was him getting ready for the tryouts. I'd have to talk to him, let him know he didn't need to do this. But not now.

I put on the headphones and snugged them into place. The sound of the bouncing basketball was gone. I opened the book to the first chapter in the last section of this unit. I pushed start on the controller, and a soft female voice began reading the chapter. My urge was to close my eyes and just listen, but that would have defeated the purpose.

I scanned down the page and started reading along. I struggled to get in sync with her. We — me and the voice — came up to the end of the first page. She paused slightly to allow me to flip the page, and we were off again. With each passing line it seemed to be getting easier. I had the strangest thought that the voice wasn't something external but was inside my head, as if I was talking to myself. She kept talking, and I kept reading. This might work.

12

COACH WILKINS TOLD me a few more details, and I wrote them down as we walked toward the center of the gym to start the tryout. Coach was nice, but he still scared me a little. I think he scared almost all of the students and a fair number of the other teachers. He was physically very big — he stood almost 6'8" — and was a former star basketball player. And, since he was born and raised in this town and went to this school, his picture and name were on awards in glass cases in the foyer and in framed pictures in the gym hallway. He still held the school records for points and assists in a season. He was the male athlete of the year in both his junior and senior year. He might have been twenty years older and forty pounds heavier than when he played, but he'd always be the high school star that took us to the state championship and went off to university — Indiana State, of course — and then went on to play semipro in Europe. People argued that he got cheated out of going pro. In Indiana, in this town, that made him a small "g" basketball god.

There were about forty-five or so guys in the gym warming up for the tryouts. Gene wasn't one of them. I hadn't spoken to him about trying out, and he hadn't spoken to me. I didn't want to embarrass him by asking. Still, I'd half expected Gene to be here, and now that he hadn't shown, I was a lot relieved and a little disappointed. He must have realized that it was impossible to get good at basketball that fast. You could learn about biology and chemistry and brain functioning, and even how to play the saxophone, sitting by yourself. You couldn't learn to play basketball by listening to it on tape or running your fingers along braille.

Coach blew his whistle, and the gym went silent.

"Okay, everybody, get your butts to the center of the gym!" he yelled, and everybody ran to comply and gathered around him. At the same time, I moved off to the side.

Then I saw Gene at the edge of the crowd. His back was to me, but his blue Jordans practically glowed. He was dressed in the pair of shorts and jersey that we'd gotten during our shopping spree. At least he could look the part, even if he couldn't play. I just hoped he wasn't doing this for me. Or maybe I secretly hoped it was for me.

Liv had continued making fun of how he followed me around. At first it was just sort of playful, but now it was starting to get on my nerves. I think she was jealous that he'd cut into our time together. She and I still studied for the SATs, but the rest of the studying I was doing with Gene. Three times this past week I'd been strapped into his contraption and studied for biology and American history. I couldn't even tell her about any of the techniques that we were using, but it did feel like the ideas were already sinking deeper into my brain.

Coach and his two assistants put the players into four groups, and they started drills. He yelled "go," and the first man in each line dribbled down the court, going full speed. Devon and Ethan were of course first in two of those lines. Each man in the four lines pulled up at the three-point line and put up a shot, and only

Devon hit. All four scrambled for their own rebound and thundered back up the court.

Gene was the last in his line. I tried to catch his eye, but I'd learned that when he was doing anything, he was laser focused. No multitasking for this guy.

The ball was passed to him, and he started dribbling down the court. He was fast, but his dribbling seemed a bit awkward, flat handed. He came up to the line, set, and shot — perfect form and nothing but net. I almost cheered, but didn't. That would have been embarrassing for both of us.

THERE WERE ONLY a few minutes left in the practice. Gene had done well. Not anywhere near saxophone spectacular, but solid. He'd run all the drills, made more than his share of shots. He did, however, look more than a little lost and out of place when they went into scrimmages. He didn't seem to really understand where he should be when he didn't have the ball, or how to play in open space, and he was shying away from contact. You couldn't get that stuff without playing against other people.

A couple of times, Devon had pulled him aside. At first, I thought it was to say something bad, but I realized he was just trying to explain a play to him. Of course, within a minute they ran a perfect pick and roll. No surprise. Gene could probably follow any directions and incorporate them immediately.

Coach blew his whistle, and everybody stopped and ran over to surround him in the center of the gym. He went on about how they'd have to "learn to work harder" and how "pain leads to gain" and about giving "a hundred and twenty-five percent." I was happy Gene didn't correct him on that being mathematically impossible, because he certainly didn't have any qualms about correcting his other teachers. Maybe he was picking up on some of the subtle social things.

"Okay, everybody, hit the showers!" he yelled.

Everybody — Gene included — headed toward the change room, some of the guys peeling off sweat-soaked T-shirts as they walked. Coach and his assistants stood and talked for a minute, and then the two of them headed to the coach's dressing room, leaving Coach alone, writing on a clipboard. I wandered over.

"Is there anything else I need to do?" I asked.

"You can head to class. Were you wondering how your boyfriend did?"

"He's not my boyfriend!"

He looked up from his clipboard. "I never see one of you without seeing the other in the halls."

"That's because I'm his host. I'm supposed to show him around the school."

"I think he knows his way around the school by now. Are you two having a little tiff?"

"A tiff?"

"A fight, an argument, a disagreement. He didn't even look in your direction the whole morning."

"He's always pretty focused no matter what he does."

"That's good. I hate players with one eye on the court and a second on the stand looking for their parents or girlfriend or friends."

"So, he did all right, right?"

"He's got a nice shot, good form, but he seems to get lost during the scrimmages. He plays a little *soft*."

I knew there wasn't much worse than being called "soft." It meant not playing with heart or being physical or determined.

"He's actually very strong."

"He looks strong, but he needs to *play* strong."

"He's never played on a team before." Maybe I shouldn't have said that.

"Homeschooled, I know."

Why had I thought Coach wouldn't know? Everybody knew everything about everybody here, and Gene seemed to be the center of a lot of gossip and a lot of social media postings.

"What he does have are active hands," Coach said. "Look at these stat lines for the scrimmage."

He turned his clipboard toward me. I recognized the names but couldn't make sense out of the jumble of initials and numbers.

"He had five deflections, three steals, and grabbed a couple of loose balls."

"But he didn't get any points, right?"

"You can't score if you don't shoot. He didn't put up a single shot in the scrimmage. These stats are even better. They're *hustle* numbers."

Anybody who knew basketball knew that hustle was as good as being soft was bad.

"I don't need another shooter. There's only one ball, and Devon and Ethan are going to take a lot of our shots. What I need is somebody to get the ball to the shooters."

"He'll get better at all of that." I realized I sounded like a friend, or a girlfriend.

"Strange you should say that. He got better with some of the drills. He seemed to be able to apply directions incredibly quickly.

It looks like he has high basketball IQ."

"Do you think he might make the team?"

"A little early to tell. That's why it's try*outs* and not a try*out*. How much do you know about basketball?"

"I live in Indiana."

He laughed. "Everybody in this state *thinks* they're an expert. Let's see if I can explain it this way. The kids in the tryout consist of three groups. There are those who are a guaranteed, sure lock for the team."

"People like Devon and Ethan."

"People like that. Those who were on the team or at least junior varsity last year. That group has locked down seven of the twelve spots on the team. Then there's a second group of fifteen or twenty guys who should just forget it and try out for the cheer squad or band."

"And the third group?"

"Those are the players who are trying out for the last four or five spots on the team." He paused. "People like your Gene."

I almost said, "He's not my Gene," but really, in some ways, he was.

"So, he does have a chance to make the team," I said.

"He won't get any serious playing time, just some spot minutes, but he could make the team. And you might want to also tell him to play with more muscle. It's basketball, not ballet."

"I'll tell him. He'll be back, and he'll be better. Guaranteed."

"Spoken like a true manager … or a girlfriend."

I was definitely the manager. Was the other something that was happening, too?

13

I DIDN'T HAVE a chance to talk to Gene before class. But then again, what was I going to say? "Coach thinks you have to stop playing so soft."

Mr. Benjamin stood at the front, and in his hands were the tests that we'd taken the previous Friday. I knew I'd done well, but I didn't want to get my hopes up too high. Although, when I was writing the test I could "hear" the female voice inside my head, pulling out the information — retrieving, as Gene would say. It seemed like Gene was also becoming the voice inside my head.

"We have a perfect paper," Mr. Benjamin said, holding it up.

There was a collective groan, and then somebody yelled, "Gene getting perfect doesn't count!"

"And what makes you think it was Gene?" Mr. Benjamin asked.

More grumbling, and a few more comments. In the short time since Gene had arrived, there was nobody in the entire school who didn't know about his academic abilities.

"There was also a ninety-three and a ninety-nine."

It was a reach for me to think I'd gotten ninety-nine, but that ninety-three was a possibility. It had to be me. Of course, that wasn't much different from what I would have gotten if I hadn't studied using Gene's techniques or simply studied for those hours while listening to music. Why didn't Mr. Benjamin just give the papers back instead of making this like he was announcing an Academy Award?

"It wasn't Gene who got one hundred," Mr. Benjamin said. "It was Becky. Can we have a round of applause for our perfect student!"

I was stunned. Big cheers and lots of clapping, the loudest coming from Gene. He had a gigantic, goofy smile on his face.

"And the ninety-nine is Gene. I'm rather disappointed in you, young man."

"Sorry, sir," Gene said. He did look genuinely sorry.

"He's joking," I said, under my breath.

"Yes, I'm joking," Mr. Benjamin repeated. "And now a word for all of you. Perhaps a few more of you might want to sit closer to the front, study a little harder, listen to my lessons a little more intentionally, or spend more time with Gene and Becky in a study group."

Or use multisensory study techniques without the use of multitasking distractions, I thought but didn't say.

Gene and I didn't really study together as much as we parallel studied. He'd set it up for me and then he'd either leave the room or sort of quietly sit and stare at the wall. At first it was a little freaky for me to have him just sitting there staring, but he explained that he had those quiet times whether I was there or not. It was, he said, his way of trying to incorporate all the new experiences, trying to bring order to his new world and the way it made him feel.

I deliberately didn't tell anybody about this sort of thing. Not even Liv. Maybe *especially* Liv. She would have made some crack about him "downloading" or being "debugged." She was relentless, and that was her biggest strength as well as her most annoying trait.

Gene told me there were times that he was overwhelmed with thoughts and feelings. I didn't believe he could be overwhelmed with thoughts, but the emotions made such great sense. How many new things was he trying to learn about? How much had changed for him in a few short weeks? And obviously it was working for him.

The strange boy in the bright blue suit who'd never been to school before was fitting in. He dressed like everybody else. He was in the school band. He was on his way to possibly being on the basketball team. His conversation was filled with normal references, and he said less that was strange. And, ever since I'd mentioned it to him, he spoke almost exclusively in contractions. It was a little thing, but it helped him to not stand out. He sounded more like a regular teenager instead of Data from *Star Trek*.

Mr. Benjamin started to hand out the papers and gave me mine. I stared down at the red *100* at the top of the top page. It practically glowed.

Gene gave me a big smile and a thumbs-up. He looked genuinely happy, almost proud. He *should* be proud. This mark was at least in part about him and what he had shown me. I'd be sure to thank him. And tell him he had to stop playing so soft.

"I WANTED TO thank you for all the help you gave me," I said to Gene as we left biology class.

"You wrote the test. I just helped facilitate a method that would allow you to study."

"But a hundred percent is like a dream. What I really can't believe is that I beat you."

"You studied very hard. You were very focused."

Then a thought came to me. I grabbed him by the arm and stopped him from walking. "I'm surprised I got perfect, but more surprised that you didn't. Are you saying you really didn't know the right answer for one of the questions?"

He hesitated before answering. "I thought that it would be nice for you to be the only person who got perfect."

"You deliberately made a mistake so I could score higher than you?"

He nodded.

"That's so ... so ..." I was going to say wrong, but I didn't. "So sweet, but you didn't have to do that. I don't want you to do that again. Wait, how did you know I was going to get perfect?"

"You studied, and you're naturally smart, so I thought you might. I hoped you might."

I threw my arms around him and gave him a big hug. I released my grip. Gene looked confused and embarrassed. He opened his mouth to speak, but no words came out.

"That's for believing in me," I said.

"No, thanks for believing in me," Gene said. "Maybe I should give you a hug."

"You could if you wanted. You know, I do believe in you. But maybe we should talk a little bit about basketball."

"How do you think I did?"

"You did well, really well, but ... Do you know what it means to play soft?"

14

THE CROWD WAS loud and angry. It was a preseason game, but it was still a basketball game and it was still Indiana and nobody liked to lose. Especially not lose so badly. We were blowing Carmel High School away. With less than three minutes to go, we were thirty-four points ahead.

The other team's coach called a time-out, and both teams ran to the benches. There was a chorus of booing, and I realized they were booing the home team and not us.

As our coaches and the rest of the team got up and huddled on the court, I stayed on the end of the bench. This really had been a team effort, but Gene had made the difference. I looked down at the score sheet in my hand.

Gene had played less than three minutes in the first quarter and hadn't taken a shot, but he had got two rebounds. In the second quarter he was in for almost six minutes, didn't take a shot, had three assists, three rebounds, and three steals. Coach said the steals were what made him put Gene in for longer in the third quarter. He got some more rebounds, some more steals, and then Coach made a decision to start running a play for him — a simple drive and kick out. Devon drove the paint, and if the double collapsed on him, he kicked it out to Ethan, who sent it to Gene for a corner three. They ran the play three times, and Gene was three for three for nine points in the third.

Then things got crazy. Gene started the fourth quarter, and they started running play after play for him. Coach had said that they'd stop running it when somebody stopped them. And they didn't. Either they doubled down on Devon and he kicked it out or they shifted toward Gene and he kept the ball for an easy path to the basket. As Coach said, they got to "pick their poison," but either way, they were going to die.

As the baskets sank and the score rose, the other team got more frustrated and more physical. They tried to muscle Devon out down low and make him pay for his baskets with hard fouls. I knew that wasn't going to work. Another guy took a shot at Gene, pushing him into the bleachers as he released his shot — which dropped. Gene picked himself up, flashed the guy a big smile, and then sank the free throw to make it a four-point shot. Gene had already gone seven for seven for twenty-two points in the *quarter*.

The ref blew his whistle, signaling the end of the time-out. All five of our starters came to the bench, and five subs went in. The lead was so great and the time so short that there was no chance of a comeback. Besides, this was preseason, and it was supposed to be about helping to decide the last roster spots more than it was about winning or losing. Now, there was no question Gene had one of those spots.

I walked down the bench and handed a towel to each of the guys who had just come off.

"Thanks," Gene said as he took the towel.

"You played well."

"Not soft?" he whispered.

"Tough," I said.

The opposition got a long three-ball, and the crowd cheered, catching our attention too. It didn't matter as the clock kept ticking down. The merciful thing was just to end before there was any more embarrassment heaped on. The final buzzer sounded. I looked at the scoreboard. Final score ninety-seven to sixty-seven. A true blowout. Within seconds, the scoreboard went blank, erasing the score. I didn't blame them.

The remaining crowd started to file out, and both teams headed for the dressing rooms to shower and change. My job now was to talk to the refs, verify the score sheets, and gather up the towels and water bottles.

"Let me help you," Gene said.

"Sorry, but basketball stars aren't supposed to pick up towels. You should join your team, celebrate, and take a shower. You *really* need a shower."

He smiled. "I did well, right?"

"You did spectacularly. I was trying to figure out how many points you would have got if you'd been shooting the whole game."

"It would have been eighty-eight points. Would you share a seat with me on the bus ride home?"

"Of course. Now, get going."

He jogged off, leaving me with the empty water bottles and the soggy, sweaty towels. Somehow that didn't seem so bad.

I STOOD IN front of the school with the wagon filled with our equipment, waiting for our bus. This was where we were dropped off, and this was where we were supposed to be picked up, wasn't it?

I felt very conspicuous in my bright red Westfield sweatshirt as blue and gold-clad Carmel High School students left the school and walked by. Most just ignored me, others gave me a sideways glance, some offered a "Good game," and a few said snarky things. I tried my best to be friendly to some and just ignore others. Not much worse than a bad loser — unless it was a bad winner.

"You guys suck!"

I jumped in shock as a guy practically pushed into my face and space and yelled. He had three friends with him. I recognized them from the bleachers behind our bench. They'd been amongst a group of the loudest, most annoying fans.

"You just got lucky!" he yelled, and his three friends laughed like a drove of donkeys.

"Yeah, the score showed how lucky we are," I said. Maybe being a bit of a bad winner wasn't so wrong.

"We could have beaten you!" a second guy screamed.

"Your team probably could have beaten *me*, but it was our *team* you couldn't beat."

A couple of girls standing to the side both laughed. That didn't seem to make the four guys any happier looking.

"That's just exhibition play! It don't mean nothing! Crawl on back to Westfield!"

People had stopped and were watching. There was a little crowd around us. Some looked amused, entertained by what was going on. Some looked as shocked as I felt, but nobody said anything.

Suddenly, one of the guys kicked the wagon, and some of the water bottles tumbled over the side.

"What are you doing?" I said.

The guy grabbed me by the arm, and I screamed.

Then, in a flash, Gene was there. He grabbed the guy by the arm and twisted it. The guy's hand released me, and he went flying over the wagon and landed on his back on the pavement. There was a collective gasp, and everybody seemed frozen in place.

"Get him!" one of the other guys yelled. He took a step forward, and Gene grabbed him by the arm and flipped him over too. The guy screamed as he flew through the air and thudded to the pavement next to his friend.

Nobody else moved. Not the other two guys. Not anybody in the crowd. The first guy Gene had tossed was now sitting up. The second was still down. He looked like the air had been knocked out of him. Gene faced the two remaining guys. His arms were up, his hands in fists, his feet apart. He looked like he was in a karate movie.

"Neither of you should do anything that's threatening," Gene said. His words were quiet and even. "I've been practicing martial arts much longer than I've played basketball, and I'm much more skilled in it."

Nobody moved. The entire crowd just silently stared.

"Help your friends up," Gene said. "And you all should leave. Now."

They edged past Gene, giving him lots of space, and around the wagon to their fallen friends. Gene shifted so that he was still standing between them and me. I bent down and picked up the fallen water bottles and put them back into the wagon. They limped away, looking over their shoulders at Gene.

"The bus couldn't get into the driveway with the traffic, so it's waiting around the corner of the school," Gene said. "That way. Go, and I'll be right behind you."

I grabbed the handle of the wagon and started off. The edge of the crowd opened up to allow me to pass, and a couple of people apologized for what had happened. Looking over my shoulder, I saw Gene still hadn't moved. Then he started, walking backward at first and then spinning around and quickly catching up with me.

"Are you all right?" he asked.

"Yes, I'm fine. Was that karate?"

"It's a form of martial arts more related to judo. It was thought it would be good for me to have that skill before I started school this year."

"So, you knew you were going to be attending here for your senior year a long time ago."

"Not that long."

"Are you saying that you just started taking lessons?" I asked.

"A while ago. I'm really not that good."

"You looked pretty good to me. Is there anything you're not good at?"

He shrugged. "Understanding basic social situations seems to be hard, and of course I have a simply *tremendous* sense of humor."

"That was almost funny."

"I'm trying. I'm a pretty fast learner."

"I guess I should just be grateful you are."

We rounded the corner of the school, and the bus was waiting.

"Are you grateful enough to go to Friday's dance?" Gene asked.

"Everybody is … Liv, Emma, Sasha, everybody. We've talked about that."

"I meant, do you want to go with me?" Gene said.

"Like a date?"

"Would that be bad?"

"Not bad. Besides, I'm your host, I have no choice but to go with you and show you around. Wait, do you know how to dance?" Before he could reply, I knew the answer. "By next Friday, you'll know how to dance, won't you?"

He smiled. "Well, is it a date?"

"It's a date."

"Like a real date?"

I nodded. "A real date." I was going to the dance. With Gene.

15

THE MUSIC WAS pounding, and the gym was packed. The
dance was a Halloween theme, and I was dressed as a bunny. It
was something I'd recycled from when I was twelve.

The whole basketball team had agreed to dress as superhe-
roes. Ethan was the Flash and Devon was the Incredible Hulk.
He'd even painted himself green. Gene was dressed as Superman.
It wasn't his idea, but the guys told him that after the last two
games, he didn't have any choice. In the second exhibition game,
he'd gotten a triple double — eleven assists, fourteen rebounds,
and thirty-nine points.

Liv leaned in close and yelled into my ear. "Gene looks good
in that Superman suit. No need for extra fake muscles, and he has
some moves."

"Not bad."

He was out on the dance floor. He had danced the first few
with me when Ella — beautiful, popular Ella — asked him to
dance. She was dressed as a cheerleader, which wasn't much of
a costume since she was a cheerleader.

Gene had agreed to dance with her, but only after he asked me
and I said it was all right. Really, it wasn't. Not for him to ask me,
not for me to say no to him, not for him to say yes, and really not
all right for her to come up and ask him to begin with. She should

have been dancing with her own date.

Her date, Nathan, was off to the side with a couple of his buddies. He was dressed as an astronaut. He didn't look any happier than I felt. I was working hard not to look upset. I was going for a casual "don't care" attitude, but I wasn't sure that was working.

"That was wrong," Liv said.

"Gene is free to dance with anybody he wants to. It's not like he's my boyfriend."

"But he is your date for the night. It's amazing how fast Gene went from blue-suited strange boy to somebody Ella wanted to dance with."

"That was pretty quick, but there's so much he still doesn't understand."

"He is *so* different," Liv said.

"Sure, he's different, but isn't everybody different?"

"Not as different as him."

"I think he could be neurologically diverse."

"Are you going to explain that?" Liv asked.

"I was doing some reading. Neurodivergent means people who have dyslexia or ADHD or autism."

"Yeah, I've heard about people who are like that," Liv said. "Sometimes they're really smart or can do complex math but can get confused around some basic things. Wasn't there some story about how Einstein couldn't find his way home?"

"The front door of his house was painted red so that he could identify his house. Before that, he often ended up in other people's places. They'd come home and find him sitting at their kitchen table," I replied.

"And you think Gene could be like that?" she asked.

"Can't you picture him doing that?"

She shrugged. "I could … I guess, but I don't know." She shook her head. "I still think he's some sort of high-tech robot or android."

"You really are unbelievable sometimes," I said.

"Or maybe I think differently. He could even be an alien."

"An alien?"

"Why not? He's so much smarter than all of us! He might be from another planet. After all, there isn't really that much intelligent life down on this planet."

"That's even more unbelievable."

"Just don't say I didn't warn you if you get kidnapped and taken to another planet. That's all I'm saying."

He wasn't an alien, but he had come a long way in less than six weeks. From dressing right to playing a solo at the last assembly to being the leading scorer in the last home game of the preseason. By the fourth quarter, the crowd had started chanting his name.

It was official. He was on the team. He was probably going to be a starter. Sometimes he hung out with Devon and Ethan and the other "cool" kids. He even could, if he wanted, have lunch with them. Instead, he still had lunch with me and the girls. That meant something. Not dancing with Ella would have meant more.

The song ended, and Gene offered Ella a little bow. He started to walk away, and she grabbed him by the arm. A slow song had started to play, and she wrapped her arms around him. He looked at me over the top of her head with an expression that said, *I'm sorry*.

"One dance was bad, two is really bad," Liv said. "Especially a slow dance."

That did make it worse.

"Maybe you should go over and tell her off," Liv said.

"I'm not going to do that!"

"I know. Then you should at least go over and cut in."

"I'm not going to do that either."

"So, what are you going to do?"

"I'm going to go and have some punch."

"Punch would be good. Come on."

Liv actually took me by the hand, and we walked around the edge of the gym. Very deliberately, I didn't look out at the dance floor. I didn't want to see them.

Liv ladled out a glass of punch for each of us.

"Too bad it isn't spiked."

I turned around. It was Nathan — Ella's date.

"I'm sure lots of people have tried," Liv said.

Mr. Benjamin was stationed by the refreshments to make sure that didn't happen.

"What do you think of our dates?" Nathan asked as he gestured to the dance floor.

I turned around. They were looking awfully comfortable out there.

"He shouldn't be dancing with her," Nathan said, answering his own question.

"*He* didn't ask *her*," I said.

"Maybe you and I should dance? You know, a little hop around the dance floor."

"I'm not dancing with somebody just to make somebody else jealous."

"I didn't mean it that way!" Nathan protested. "I just want to dance."

"Dance with Liv. I'm going out for some air."

I put down my plastic glass and went for the door, not looking back at him or Liv and certainly not at the dance floor. The music faded as the gym door swung shut, and I walked down the hall. I looked straight ahead, not at anybody else in the corridor. I just wanted to get outside, to be alone and … I felt my chin start to quiver. I was about to start crying. How stupid, how emotional.

I went through the side door and into the parking lot. There were a dozen people off to the left side vaping or smoking. I turned away from them. The tears felt like they were closer, and I certainly didn't want anybody to see me cry. I just couldn't figure out why it made me feel so sad. He wasn't my boyfriend. He was just some —

"Becky!"

I turned. Gene was jogging across the parking lot toward me. I tried hard to snuffle back the tears and wiped my sleeve across my face.

"Liv said you were upset and … are you crying?" he asked.

"I'm not crying … allergies."

"You don't have any allergies."

"How do you know that?"

He shrugged. "I know I shouldn't have danced with her," he said.

"I told you that you could."

"I didn't understand that it didn't matter what you said, that it was wrong."

"And now you do know?" I asked.

"Liv walked out onto the gym floor, dragged me away from Ella, and explained it to me. She told me I was an idiot and to stop acting like an alien life-form."

"Yeah, you are an idiot."

He laughed. I hadn't expected that. "I'm sorry I hurt your feelings and that I made you cry. I just didn't know. Social nuances are my kryptonite."

I chuckled. "That was both a joke and a social reference. Not bad."

"So much of this social stuff confuses me. I didn't know it would hurt you, or I never would have done it."

"You should know you don't have to hang out with me and the girls anymore."

"I don't understand."

"You don't have to go to dances with me. You can go with anybody you want, including Ella."

"I don't want to go with Ella."

"Why not? She's beautiful."

"She's *very* beautiful," he said.

I hadn't expected that.

"She has all the characteristics that are considered to constitute beauty in our society."

"Is that scientific fact?" I asked.

"No, it's according to *People*, *Vanity Fair*, *Entertainment Tonight*, and *TMZ*."

I couldn't help but laugh. "That's right, you are doing your research."

"But she's not as beautiful as you," Gene said.

"Yeah, right."

"You *are* more beautiful."

"Not according to *Entertainment Tonight* or *People*. Look, if you want to dance with Ella or have lunch with her or take her to the next dance, that's your decision."

"I don't want to do any of those things." He paused and opened his mouth to speak and then didn't. He took a deep breath. "I'm not in love with her."

"I didn't say you were in love with …" Wait, what was he saying?

"I'm in love with you."

I felt my whole body go flush.

"I'm in love with you," he repeated.

"You can't be in love with me."

"I am. I've lost my appetite. I have trouble sleeping. I can't concentrate. My body tingles when I'm around you."

"That sounds like the flu."

"I can't stop thinking about you. When I'm not around you, all I want to do is be around you."

"But we've only known each other for a few weeks."

"I knew after the first week. I think I knew the first day. Don't you believe in love at first sight?"

"I wasn't in love with you at first sight." He looked hurt. "I mean, I don't believe in that. It's just that I was the first girl you got to know, that's all." Maybe the first girl in his entire life.

"You make it sound like I'm a newborn chick imprinting on the first object it sees."

We'd taken all of that in biology.

"Gene, we haven't even kissed."

"I've thought about kissing you … a lot. Have you thought of kissing me?"

I didn't answer. I had.

"Would it be all right if I … if we kissed?"

I nodded my head ever so slightly.

"I've never kissed anybody," he said.

"Never?"

He shook his head. "Homeschooled, remember? It was either nobody or my mother."

I couldn't help but laugh.

"Have you kissed a lot of people?" Gene asked.

"A couple. I've been on dates."

"This is my first date," he said. "So many firsts."

He took a hand and put it under my chin, raising my head slightly. With the fingers of his other hand, he gently brushed my cheeks, removing the traces of the tears.

"I didn't think our first kiss would be in the parking lot with me dressed like a bunny and you dressed like Superman."

"So, you *have* been thinking about kissing me."

I shrugged. "A little."

"I'm glad it wasn't just me." He leaned forward and gently kissed me. It was soft and sweet, and my whole body tingled.

He leaned back. "Well?"

"It was nice."

"I was hoping for more than nice," Gene said.

"It was better than nice. Did you do some research on kissing?"

"I watched movies with first kisses."

"You are, as always, a fast learner." I paused. "Although practice makes perfect."

I went up on my tiptoes, and this time I kissed him. And then I understood, slowly, but then all at once.

16

WE WERE EATING in the dining room instead of the kitchen, and my mother had insisted that we use the good dishes and the silver serving set. I straightened the forks and knives. I couldn't believe how nervous I felt. I'd never had a boyfriend over for dinner, and there was no telling what my father might say. Not that he wasn't a good guy — he was a *very* good guy — but sometimes words just popped out of his mouth. I had to hope that today the filters would be in place. Maybe I could nudge him in the right direction.

"Dad, do you think that tonight you could —"

"Try not to say anything to embarrass you?"

I nodded.

"You know I never try to embarrass anybody."

"I was just hoping that today you could *really* try *not* to embarrass me. Or Gene. He's different."

"He's a seventeen-year-old boy, so he's not that different. The only things a boy in Indiana is thinking about are basketball, burgers, beer, and babes."

"So, now I'm a babe?"

"You're my daughter. I have to keep an eye on him."

"But weren't you once a seventeen-year-old boy in Indiana? Are you telling me that Mom was a babe?"

"A big-time babe," my mother said as she walked into the room carrying a serving bowl. "That's why he started dating me."

She gave him a big kiss. They were like that. It was sweet and a little bit embarrassing all at once.

"First off, Gene isn't from here, and he doesn't eat meat of any kind, so burgers are out, and he doesn't drink anything, including beer."

"That just leaves basketball and babes to fill his head. That's even worse," my father said.

"He's not like that. You'll see."

"His parents are both doctors, right?" he asked.

"Research doctors."

"And you mentioned that they're both geniuses," my mother added.

"So is Gene."

"He's not going to be uppity because I'm only a heating and cooling contractor, is he?"

"Of course not!" I knew that wasn't true of some of the kids at our school. I felt bad that I didn't usually tell anybody what my father did for a living.

"Because I don't know any geniuses that can fix a furnace or an air conditioner," he said.

"Just give him a chance." I paused. I knew what I wanted to say but was unsure how to say it. "Sometimes he can be a little, um, awkward around new people."

My mother laughed. "Sounds like somebody I know. Actually, sounds like somebody I married. Do you remember the first time you met my parents?" she asked my father.

"I'd like to forget," my father said. He looked embarrassed.

"I've never heard that story. Tell me, please."

"Well, for starters he was twenty-five minutes late."

"I wasn't late getting to your house, I just had to build up my nerve to knock."

"My parents saw him walking back and forth in front of our house, and my father asked if he was 'too dumb to find the door.'"

"He said that?" my father asked.

"He did. And then when your father did come in, he tripped on his own feet and crashed into my mother when he was walking over to shake her hand and they both almost fell over."

"It wasn't my most graceful moment, but I won them over."

"It took years, but eventually even my father learned to love him."

"That's because I am quite lovable," he said.

"Yes, you are," I agreed. "Just give Gene a chance."

The doorbell rang.

"Apparently, he found the door," my mother said. "And he's on time."

"Very funny."

"Please, Dad."

"I'll try," my father said.

I went to the door, and they trailed behind. Gene stood at the door, a big bouquet of flowers in his hands. He handed the flowers to my mother — I had thought they were for me, but this was better.

"That was so kind!" My mother beamed.

He and my father shook hands. "Good to meet you, son," my father said.

"It's a pleasure to meet you, sir. Thank you for inviting me to your home for dinner."

"We thought it was about time," my father said. "After all, this is my little girl, and like I've always said, I'm not afraid to go back to jail."

"You've been in jail?" Gene asked.

"Of course, he hasn't!" I exclaimed. "It's a joke by his favorite comedian."

Gene turned to me. "Is that a dad joke?"

"Exactly!" I exclaimed.

"Please, come in and sit down," my mother offered. "Supper will be ready in less than fifteen minutes."

She led the way into the living room, and Gene sat down beside my mother and across from my father. I kept standing.

"I was reading about the basketball team. You're off to a good start," my father said.

There'd been a story about the team in the *Nobleton Examiner*, our local newspaper, and there was a nice picture of Gene putting up a shot as part of the article.

"Yes, sir."

"And it looks like you're having a *great* start," my father said.

"It isn't about individual numbers. It's a team game."

My father laughed. "That's the way it should be."

"There's no 'I' in 'team,' sir. The great players know that."

"And just exactly who do you think is a great one?"

"Indiana's own Larry Bird was the best at making his teammates better," Gene said.

My father jumped to his feet and reached out his hand, and the two shook hands again. "Nice to see a young person who understands what the game is really about."

"Coach has helped me understand. And, of course, your daughter. She knows a lot about sports. She taught me how to bowl last weekend."

"You never bowled before?" my father asked.

"No, sir."

"And how did you do?"

"My first game was a one-ten."

"Not bad for a beginner," my father said sympathetically.

"And in his third game he scored two-seventy-five," I added.

"Two-seventy-five! That's either amazing or amazingly lucky."

"Probably just beginner's luck. Do you bowl, sir?"

"Does a bear crap in the woods?" my father asked.

Gene just looked confused.

"He means, yes, he does bowl," I answered.

"Would you like to go bowling sometime, sir?" Gene asked.

"That would be nice. Let's set a time. Maybe we can even bring the girls."

"Do you mean the babes?" I asked.

My father shot me a dirty look, and my mother jumped to the rescue.

"How about if everybody washes up and we'll be ready to eat."

I guessed I should have been grateful — well, as grateful as you could be when your boyfriend and your father were setting up a playdate.

17

THE LAST OF the audience had almost gone, leaving the gym nearly quiet as I gathered up the towels, put away the balls, and put the nets up. The bleachers had been completely filled, and all the standing room had been taken as well. It had been so loud during the game that I thought the roof might blow off. It wasn't just students and teachers — lots of people from town had come out to watch. There were rumors that there were a few university and college scouts in the audience. They were there to watch the game but mainly to see Devon, Ethan, and Gene play.

It was a great game. We'd won by twenty-seven points for our fifth win in a row. Gene had been spectacular. The crowd chanted his name, and there had been signs that said *Gene, Gene the Shooting Machine*. He had thirty-seven points, shooting nine of ten from the field and ten for ten from the line. All through the preseason and now into the regular games he seemed to be getting better and better. Sometimes it felt like he was improving each *quarter*.

Scouting reports were just part of basketball, and our opponents had obviously heard about Gene. They knew they had to shut him down and stop him from shooting. They tried, and they failed. He could get his shot up so quickly and from so many angles that no one player could cover him close enough to shut him down. Then when they doubled him, he just passed the ball to the open man. Devon had twenty-nine points, most of them assisted by Gene.

Then the fouls started. I thought at first it was just players being frustrated, but it became obvious it was a coaching strategy. They thought they could hard foul him to get him off his game, but that didn't work any better than the double-teams. He just picked himself up and then made the free throw. He didn't even react, didn't give them the courtesy of even allowing them to think they were getting to him. Well, at least until the end.

With just over five minutes left in the game, the player who had been giving him the hardest time was going up for a meaningless layup. Gene came out of nowhere and gave him a really hard foul. He was given a flagrant foul, and Coach decided to take him out of the game. The crowd gave him a standing ovation, and each player and the coach gave him a high five as he came to the bench. So much for playing soft.

Gene was now a basketball player. That's how people saw him. He had changed the way he dressed to look more like the rest of the team instead of so preppy. He was talking like them. He'd even changed the way he walked. It was more of a swagger. And I knew the changes were deliberate. Gene had not only told me what he was doing but also asked my opinion about the changes. He was treating all of this with the same deliberate focus that he put into studying. That he put into everything.

"Excuse me."

I looked up. It was a man in a blue and red tracksuit. I'd seen him in the audience, standing off to the side during the game. He looked like an athlete. Or a police officer. He had short hair and was thick and muscular looking. His eyes were hidden behind dark sunglasses. Why would he be wearing sunglasses indoors?

"You're the team manager, Becky, right?"

"Um, yes. Why?"

"I was wondering if you have a few minutes to answer some questions."

"What sort of questions?" I asked nervously. Something about him made me feel anxious. I looked past him and was relieved to see a couple of people still sitting in the bleachers.

"Questions about the game," he said.

"Are you a reporter?"

"No, I'm a scout." He'd lowered his voice like he was telling me a secret. "I can't really tell you what university I'm from. Enough to say it's a fairly prestigious program."

"Coach will be out of his office soon."

"I will talk to him, but I was hoping to get your perspective too. I've always found that team managers see things that others might not notice. I imagine that you do know the game, am I correct?"

"I guess I do."

"And being there for every game and every practice gives you a unique perspective that even the coach doesn't notice."

"I'm not sure about that," I said.

"Don't sell yourself short. I'm particularly interested in one player. Gene Newman."

Wow, a basketball scout from a big-time program was here to watch Gene play.

"He had a pretty amazing game," he said.

"He did, and the thing is that he's getting better game by game."

I could be a manager and also be his girlfriend. I'd talk him up.

"Indiana is my territory, so I know all the up-and-coming players, but I've never even heard of him before this season."

"He's not from Indiana. He just moved here this year."

"Still, somebody that good should be on the national radar of scouts. Is he from another country or something?"

I laughed, thinking that Liv thought he might be from another planet. "No, he's just from New York."

"New York City produces a lot of quality players."

"No, he's from a little town upstate."

"Do you know the name of it?" he asked.

"It's called Plattsburgh." I wondered why he'd asked that.

"I've heard of Plattsburgh, but I haven't heard of him. Do you know what high school team he played on there?"

"He didn't play high school ball. He didn't even go to high school before this," I explained.

"Then he must have played for some incredibly good community teams."

"He never played on a community team either," I answered, and then thought, *Should I be telling him any of this? Why did he even want to know?* Then again, he was a scout, and I guessed he just wanted as much information as possible. That's what scouts did, right? And I wasn't going to miss a chance to make Gene look good.

"So, what you're seeing is only the beginning of how good he could become … how good he *will* become," I said, boosting him further. "He's just a really, really fast learner. It's almost unbelievable how fast he learns things."

"I imagine he must have an incredibly high basketball IQ. In fact, he must be one very smart guy in general."

"He is! He's the smartest person I've ever met."

It felt like I was bragging or talking him up or sounding like a girlfriend, but I meant everything I said. And saying it to a university basketball scout was only going to help.

"It sounds like you know him very well," he said.

"I do. I was assigned to be his host when he came to our school, and he's my, um, friend."

He smiled. "Sounds like it's a little more than just being a friend."

I felt myself blushing.

The first of the players came out of the dressing room.

"If there are no more questions, I have to finish cleaning up," I said.

"No, I think I have everything I need. I better get going too."

"But didn't you want to talk to Coach?"

He looked at his watch. "Maybe the next time. Thank you so much, Becky, you've been more helpful than you can even know. And could you do me a favor?"

"What?"

"I'm competing for prospects against other scouts. You know how competitive scouting can be. So, if you could keep this conversation quiet, I'd appreciate it."

He turned and left before I could answer. Was that why he was wearing the shades, so he could try to go unnoticed or unrecognized? It didn't really matter. I was definitely going to tell people about it. Especially Gene.

Gene came out of the dressing room. He walked over and gave me a hug and a kiss on the cheek.

"You look beautiful," he said.

"You say that all the time."

"That's because you're beautiful all the time."

He was always giving me compliments. I was also pretty sure he'd researched what it meant to be a good boyfriend. He hadn't told me, but sometimes it felt like we were in an internet questionnaire that might have been titled "How good is your boyfriend?" He opened doors, held chairs, complimented my hair, got me flowers, and bought me a stuffed animal. It could have seemed phony or artificial, but he made it all seem natural.

"Excuse me," a little grade nine student asked. "Could I have your autograph?"

He held out a pen and a pad toward Gene.

"You want his autograph?" I asked.

He nodded. "I want to be able to show it to people, you know, when he's in the NBA."

Gene looked at me as if he wanted my approval before proceeding.

"Why not?" I asked.

He took the pad and pen.

"And could you also put 'To my number one fan, Colby.'"

Gene signed it and handed it back.

"Thanks. Do you think we could do a selfie together?"

"Better yet, give me the phone and I'll take it," I said.

Colby handed me the phone. They posed, and I took a few shots and gave him back his phone. Colby thanked Gene again, and then he took off, yelling to his friends that he'd "got it."

"I've never signed an autograph before," Gene said.

"You better get used to it if you keep playing like you've been playing."

"That won't happen," he said.

I gave him a questioning look.

"I'm going to keep getting better."

With anybody else, that might have sounded like bragging. With Gene, it was just a factual statement. The same statement I'd just made to the scout.

I shouldn't have been surprised there had been a scout here to see him. Gene had already been mentioned on a couple of basketball websites, and there was a highlight clip of him on You-Tube. Those things had probably been what had gotten the scout's attention, and there was no way wearing sunglasses was going to keep Gene a secret. In a place where basketball was king, Gene was the new prince in waiting, which sort of made me, as his girlfriend, a princess. That was strange — me, a princess.

"Oh, that reminds me, I was approached by a scout."

"What sort of scout?" Gene asked.

I couldn't believe he didn't understand what that meant, but then again, it probably wasn't something he'd ever heard about.

"College and university teams send out people, talent scouts, to watch games. If they think you have potential, they make you an offer. This guy seemed pretty interested in you."

"What was he interested in? What did he ask you? What did you say about me?" He sounded uneasy.

"Relax, I told him you were an international spy."

"But why would you tell him that?" he exclaimed.

"Gene, come on. We talked about basketball. What else would a basketball scout be interested in?"

"Oh, sure, of course."

"I'm so glad your basketball skills have developed faster than your sense of humor, or the team would be in *serious* trouble," I said. "He wanted to know about your playing. He sounded pretty interested. If you're lucky, he could offer you a free ride."

"A free ride to where?"

I couldn't help but chuckle. If he didn't know about scouts, why would he know about a "free ride"?

"You could play basketball and go to school completely for free — a free ride. Then again, with your marks, you could go to any school in the country on an academic scholarship. Have you thought about where you want to go?"

"Not really."

"You could go to Harvard or Yale or Oxford or anywhere you wanted."

"Do they have basketball teams?"

"Sure … Well, probably not Oxford. They'd have a rowing team. But they're like the Ivy League schools — none of them are what you'd call basketball schools. Kentucky or North Carolina, Duke, UCLA, or Indiana are basketball schools."

"You'd like to go to Indiana, correct?" he asked.

"It's at the top of my list."

"I should go to Indiana, too."

For a split second I wondered if that scout was from Indiana. That would make sense since he'd said this was his territory.

"Indiana's a great university, but it's not Harvard. Nothing is Harvard. If they offer you a scholarship, that's where you should go. That's where I'd go."

"Then why aren't you going to Harvard?"

"Yeah, like I can get into Harvard."

"Why couldn't you?"

"Only the very best students even apply, and then only six percent of them are accepted. You need to have a grade point average of four point one and an SAT score of something around fourteen-sixty or better."

"You could do that. I believe in you."

"Not that long ago, you believed that a blue suit was the best thing to wear to school." I felt bad for saying it. "Look, I appreciate your faith in me, I really do." I squeezed his hand tighter. "But I don't have the marks or the money. Do you know what tuition is at Harvard?"

"I don't know what tuition is anywhere."

"Sixty-three thousand dollars for tuition, room, and board."

"If you weren't thinking of applying, how do you know what it would cost?" Gene asked.

"Well, I looked it up, for fun, because I was sort of curious."

"Then you *are* interested in going to Harvard."

"It doesn't matter. Like I said, I don't have the marks or the money."

"You could. Let me study for the SATs with you."

"I study with Liv."

"You could study with both of us separately. It would increase your SAT score the way it's elevated your marks."

My marks had come up almost eight percent. If I could increase my SATs by the same percentage, I'd be pretty close to the top.

"Will you think about it?" he asked.

"There just isn't enough time. The test is in two weeks."

"That's more time than you'd need. We could start tonight."

"If I stayed in your room twenty-four-seven for the next four-teen days wearing those headphones, I couldn't get my marks that high."

He took me gently by the arm, looked around, and walked me to the far corner of the gym. What was he doing?

"There are other things," he said, his voice barely a whisper. He looked all around again as if he was nervous somebody was listening. "There are things I haven't told you. *Top secret* things."

"Then you shouldn't tell me. I don't want to get you in trouble."

"I don't care," he said. "You could raise your score by one hundred points."

"In two weeks? That's impossible."

"It isn't. Believe me. I want you to go to Harvard with me. I don't want to be apart from you because —"

I held up my finger, and he stopped. We had an agreement that he wasn't going to use the L-word. I just wasn't ready to hear it or say it back. It actually scared me.

"Can we talk about this later?" I asked. "I really have to finish cleaning up."

"I can help you clean up, and I really can raise your score. Just think about it, okay?"

"I'll think about, but not right now."

18

WE WALKED INTO the cafeteria. It was always such a happy place the day after a victory. People turned to watch us — or to watch Gene. Funny, he was still the center of attention, just like he had been when he first got to the school, but now it was for such different reasons.

Off to one side sat Devon, some of the other basketball guys, and their assorted friends and girlfriends. There was a standing invitation for us to join them. Gene gave a little salute, and they yelled back greetings.

Devon started a chant of "Gene, Gene, Gene" and some others joined in. I had to hand it to Devon. He could have been upset about all the attention Gene was getting, but he wasn't. Of course, it didn't hurt that the scouts who would come to see Gene would also see him play.

Liv and the girls waved to us as we came across the room. The girls all gave me and Gene a hug. They congratulated him on having a great game.

"It was like you were playing out of this world," Liv said.

I knew that was more than a compliment. It was a gentle dig about Gene being an alien.

"Really, the way you were scoring, it was like you were a machine — you know, a robotic shooting machine."

I gave her a dirty look, which she saw and ignored.

"I guess we won't know anything until we look at all the *data.*"

A further reference to Data from *Star Trek* and Gene being an android.

"The other team couldn't find a way to delete your ability to —"

"Stop it," I snapped. "Stop it now."

She shot me a defiant look. This was becoming more and more an issue between us. My mother had even noticed and said she thought Liv was jealous that Gene was taking up my time and felt left out.

"What did the doctor have to say about your scan?" Liv asked.

I felt relieved to talk about something different.

I'd gone for the results of the latest one yesterday afternoon. "Everything is good."

"Not surprising. You haven't had a headache for weeks," Liv said.

"Almost seven weeks."

"Then why are you still going for scans?" Sasha asked.

I shrugged. "It was scheduled. There's another one scheduled in three weeks."

"You really should cancel that one," Gene said.

"What?" I asked.

"The headaches are gone. It probably was just tension and stress."

"You should still go," Liv said. "It's important to follow up just to be on the safe side."

"Liv's right. It doesn't hurt to follow up," I said.

"But you don't like them, and it's really not needed, and you're exposing yourself to unnecessary —"

"The girl can do what she wants," Liv said. "This is her life. Not yours or mine."

It was just a simple statement, but it made me feel better. I was used to Liv always being in my corner.

"Liv's right. I'm going to go."

"Isn't that sweet, the two lovebirds are fighting," Sasha said, and the girls laughed. I wasn't finding this funny.

"Lovebirds?" Gene asked.

"It's a saying," I said.

"About birds that love each other," Liv explained. "And birds of a feather should stick together."

"We're not birds," Gene said. "And I don't want to talk about this anymore."

He stood up, grabbed his bag, turned, and walked away.

I sat there, too stunned to speak. I watched as he walked, head down, not talking or looking at anybody, across the cafeteria and out through a side door that led to the parking lot.

"Wow," Liv said.

"He looked pretty upset," Sasha said.

I jumped to my feet and ran after him. I pushed out the door and went to call his name, but he wasn't there. There were other students, walking or standing by their cars, but Gene was no-where to be seen.

"Where did he go?"

I turned. It was Liv, standing at the door. She'd come after me.

"I don't see him."

"He looked like he was going to cry, and that would be bad because —"

"Because it would get his circuitry wet or cause a malfunction in his hardware!" I snapped.

"No, because I don't like to see anybody cry, and he's a nice guy."

"It's just that … well … you know."

"I do, and sometimes I should just shut up. Sometimes I get carried away. Sorry."

"Thank you for saying that."

"I'll do better. Yell at me if I don't," she said.

"I will. I just don't understand why he's so upset right now," I said.

"I think it's because you were called lovebirds," Liv said.

"Why would that upset him?"

"How many times has he told you he loves you?" she asked. "And the only answer you give him is, 'Let's not talk about it.' How would you feel if you told somebody you loved them and that's all they said in return?"

"But he's always so logical, so smart."

"Smart has nothing to do with the heart. Feelings and emotions aren't exactly his strengths. He's probably confused."

She was right. She was the one calling him a robot or an android, but I was the one treating him like he really was one.

"You've hurt his feelings. You should find him and tell him that you love him."

"I can't do that."

"Why not? It's obvious you do."

She was right; I did love him. Slowly and then all at once it had happened. But I wasn't ready to say it. Thinking it and saying it out loud were very different things.

"Just tell him. Do you want to risk losing him?"

"I'll talk to him."

The five-minute bell sounded, and I jumped. "I have to get to English."

"Look, you could call him or even send him a text."

"You want me to tell him I love him in a text?"

"Better than not saying it."

"I'll tell him in person, but I have a presentation in English. I've got American history with him after that. Maybe we can cut class and go someplace and talk."

"Cut class?" Liv asked. "I never thought I'd hear you suggest that. It must really be love."

Maybe it is, I thought, but I didn't want to say anything out loud. I didn't want to hurt him. And I didn't want to lose him.

19

GENE DIDN'T SHOW up for American history. And then he didn't show up for basketball practice. Coach wasn't happy about people missing practice even when they had a good reason and had cleared it with him. Just not showing up was something that he *hated*. I covered by telling Coach that Gene had gone home because he wasn't feeling well.

I had no idea where he was, though. I'd tried calling him after he disappeared from the cafeteria, but he wasn't answering his phone. And I'd called a dozen times as I was walking to his house, which was now only a few blocks ahead.

He could choose to not answer his phone, but he couldn't stop me from marching up the path, knocking on the door, telling his parents I needed to talk to him, and — and what if they refused to answer the door, or he told them he didn't want to talk to me?

There was one other way. He could choose to not answer his phone or even to open the door, but I could guarantee he'd have to see me.

I WAS TAKING a shortcut through the field. The corn was so tall that I was completely hidden between the rows. Liv and Sarah and I used to play hide-and-go-seek out in the corn all the time. It was a good place to hide, and it felt good to be hidden. Being around Gene the last few weeks had made me much more visible than I was used to being. At first it was because I was with the guy in the blue suit. Then it was because he was the saxophone-playing, basketball star cool kid.

I came up to the fence between this farm and Gene's place. It was more than six feet tall and was topped by three strands of barbed wire. I moved along the fence until I found a spot where the ground was eroded and there was a gap. Leading with one arm, then my head, and rotating my shoulders, I squeezed through the gap. I stood up and brushed myself off.

Up ahead, Gene's house rose over the weeds. I could see the big tree that sat beside it. I knew his bedroom window was hiding up there amongst the branches and leaves. I slipped into the space between the garage and the old workshop. I was as hidden here as I had been in the cornfield. Somehow it seemed like it was a good idea not to be seen. The only window on this side would be Gene's bedroom, and I still couldn't see it.

I put my hands against the tree and looked up — way up. It seemed taller, and it definitely was thicker. Was that first branch now too high for me to even reach? Maybe it would be better to just go to the front door and knock. It would certainly be easier, but it wouldn't be better if he didn't answer the door.

I jumped up and wrapped my hands around the lowest branch. I pulled myself up and got a leg over and sat on the branch. Almost instantly, the leaves hid me from view. It felt like I was in a soft, safe green envelope. I started climbing.

I remembered climbing the tree, but I'd forgotten how much I'd never really liked climbing it. It made me scared back then, and

I was scared now. Thank goodness I was more than halfway up, and there were only a few more branches to go.

I climbed higher and higher until I was level with Gene's window. I peered through the leaves and into Gene's room, but I couldn't see him. He could be anywhere in the house. Wait, he might not even be home. If he wasn't, how long would I wait, and what would I say to his parents if they discovered me sitting in his room?

I shifted around, still with one arm wrapped around the trunk, and inched along, closer and closer, focused on the branch beneath my feet. I could feel it shaking and sagging beneath my weight. I shifted my grip, took another step, and reached out and grabbed the frame of the open window. I was right there, just a long step or a short leap away — or a big drop down. I took a deep breath and jumped through the window and into his room, landing on the floor and on my face.

"Becky!"

Gene was right there at my side. He helped me as I struggled to my feet.

"I hope you don't mind me dropping in."

I tried to sound casual and funny and not like some stalker girl who'd climbed a tree and leaped in his bedroom window.

"I wanted to surprise you. I bet you're surprised, right?"

"Definitely surprised."

"Sorry, I was afraid that you wouldn't answer the door if you knew it was me."

"Why wouldn't I answer the door, especially for you?" Gene asked.

"You didn't answer my calls or texts."

"Oh, my phone is in my backpack. I haven't looked at it for hours. Sorry."

"I thought you didn't answer because you're upset with me." I took a deep breath. "Because, you know, I haven't told you how I feel about you."

"You didn't have to tell me. I know you love me."

I laughed. "You seem pretty confident."

"I've noted your pupil dilation, heart palpitations, looking at me when you don't think I'm looking at you," he said. "I'm confident in the science."

"I get most of those symptoms when I run too far too fast, and I *definitely* don't even like running."

He took both my hands in his hands. "I know how you feel."

I felt my heart race — palpitate — and I wondered if my pupils had just dilated. He deserved to hear the words. "Gene Newman, I love you."

"Just as my scientific observations indicated."

"That's not the response you're supposed to give when some-body tells you they love you for the first time."

He smiled. "Becky, I love you."

He pulled me closer, but instead of kissing me he wrapped his arms around me and squeezed me tightly. I hugged him back. It felt good and warm and safe.

"I don't ever want to let you go," he whispered in my ear.

"I'm sorry for hurting your feelings by not saying it back before, not telling you I loved you."

Still holding my hands, he looked directly into my eyes. "It was wonderful to hear you say it, but you not saying it didn't hurt my feelings. I knew you needed time."

"Then why did you run out of the cafeteria and leave school?"

"It's what was said about lovebirds always being together."

"But it's just a saying, a stupid saying," I protested. "And we *are* together."

"Now, but not always."

"University is a long time from now, and we could still go to the same school."

"Us being apart could happen sooner. Much sooner. Maybe it would even be better." He looked guilty and sad and scared all rolled into one.

"What are you saying? Or what *aren't* you saying?"

"I don't know for sure yet," he said. He led me over, still holding my hand, and we sat on the edge of his bed.

"There has been discussion that the work we came to Nobleton to do is complete."

"Wait, are you saying you and your family are going to move away?" I gasped.

He nodded.

"Just tell your parents you can't move. I don't think Coach would even *allow* you to move. He could talk to them. I bet Coach and his wife would offer to let you stay with them."

"I wouldn't be allowed to stay."

"Why not? You're almost eighteen. I'm sure your parents would agree if you have a plan."

"A plan?" He laughed. "You have no idea what the plan really is. Besides, it isn't my parents' decision whether I stay or go."

"Then whose decision is it?"

"I haven't been completely honest with you."

"I understand. You've never been allowed to be completely

honest with me because some things are top secret."

"Not *top* secret. *Ultra*-secret. Ultra-secret is two levels above top secret. There would be only a few dozen people in the entire country who have that level of clearance. People like the heads of certain government agencies and, of course, the president."

"The president of the United States?"

"Yes, he would have been briefed on this project."

"Project? I don't understand … and you know the president?"

"I've been told he has knowledge of the project. He knows *about* me." He paused. "It's you who doesn't know what I am."

"I know who you are."

"You know *who* I am, but you don't know *what* I am."

"I know you're supersmart and it's because of the research your parents are doing."

"That's only part of it. There are other techniques, procedures that can enhance human intelligence. We have an MRI scanner in the laboratory in our basement."

"Why would you have that?"

"Because my brain has been scanned every week since I was born."

"But why would they do that?"

"To keep a constant record of the structure of my brain and the changes within it."

"What sort of changes?" I asked.

"Nodes and centers can enlarge or contract. Wiring can be altered. Neurons or neuron density can be magnified, and —"

There was a loud crashing sound, and I startled. Both Gene and I jumped up off the bed.

"What was that?" I asked.

There was another sound. Was it fireworks? Why would there be fireworks? Especially because it sounded like it was coming from inside the house. Had something gone wrong in the laboratory? Were there other things besides an MRI scanner down there in the basement? There was another sharp crack.

"That sounded like gunfire," I said.

"You have to stay here."

I didn't argue. Gene went to the door and threw it open. He rushed out and closed the door behind him, and I was alone. Whatever was happening was outside that door, down the stairs, and — I heard the sound of heavy footfalls coming up the stairs. Suddenly the door burst open, and Gene came back in, slamming the door behind him.

"Get in the closet," Gene hissed. "You have to hide. Get in the closet, right now! Don't argue. Now!"

20

I RAN TO the closet as Gene grabbed the dresser and pushed it against the bedroom door and then flung himself against it. There was a crash and the door pushed slightly open, and Gene pushed harder.

I stood at the closet, half in, unable to believe what was playing out before my eyes. There was another crash, and the door cracked at the top. Gene was bumped backward as the door pushed against the dresser.

He looked directly at me. "Hide … please," he whispered.

I ducked all the way into the closet and pulled the door closed. I cowered away, pushing myself into the farthest corner. There was a little bit of light leaking out from under the door and through the keyhole, but not enough to see anything. I felt around with my hands and came across the field hockey stick. I pulled it forward, holding it like a shield or a weapon.

There was a loud crash and then voices — male voices. It sounded like two or three of them. And there was the sound of footsteps and struggling and grunts and groans. What I couldn't see with my eyes I could see in my head. Somebody had forced their way, and there was a fight — somebody was fighting with Gene.

Then there was silence. That was even scarier. I was paralyzed with fear, but I needed to see, I needed to look. I needed to know if Gene — my Gene — was all right. I heard a voice, male, so soft that I couldn't make out the words.

I slowly lowered myself to my knees and positioned myself so that I could see through the keyhole. Gene was sitting on the edge of the bed, and the men were standing on either side of him, their backs to me. They were large with short hair and tracksuits. One of them turned slightly, and I realized he was holding a gun.

Gene looked calm. How could he be calm?

"We need the combination to get into the lab!" one of the men yelled.

This was a robbery, a home invasion!

"I don't know what —"

He slapped Gene across the face. I almost screamed in shock, but I choked back the reaction.

"What is the combination?" the man demanded.

"I told you I don't know."

He slapped Gene again, and I almost felt it from across the room and through the door. I had to get help. I slumped slightly down and pulled out my phone. I'd call the police. The phone glowed. I pushed the phone icon and went to dial 911 when I realized that I had no bars — no service. The closet was a dead zone. I couldn't call from here, and I couldn't very well go out into the room by the window to call.

"One way or another, we're going to get into the lab and get the serum!" he yelled.

He drew back his hand to strike Gene, and the other man grabbed his arm and held it in place, then took his gun and placed it on the windowsill.

"Leave him alone."

There was a calmness to his voice. And something familiar.

"We don't want to hurt you," the second man said. His voice was quiet. "Gene, all we want is the serum."

Serum. That was the second time I'd heard that word. What serum?

"How do you know about the serum?" Gene asked.

"We know everything about the Genesis project."

Gene had just mentioned a project, and now they were talking about it.

"We know about the project," the man said. "We know about *you.*"

"Where are my parents?"

"If by your parents you mean Dr. Lawrence and Dr. Wilson, they had to be neutralized."

That was such a strange way of saying that — "If by your parents you mean." I knew he was adopted, but they were still his parents. Weren't they?

"Where are they?" Gene asked again.

"We're not violent people, but they forced us to use violence. We can use it again. Please don't deny that you can access the lab." He paused. "You know that there is an alternate way we can get the serum." He placed a finger against the side of Gene's head. "We can simply kill you, have an autopsy performed, and extract samples of the serum from your brain."

I couldn't believe what he had just said. They were talking about killing Gene and getting something — this serum — from his brain.

"That won't work," Gene said. "There's nothing to extract."

"You might be right," the man said. "Although it won't do you any good. You'll be dead and gone. Just get us into the lab."

"And if I do?" Gene asked. "What's to stop you from just killing me then?"

"You have my word that we will leave you, albeit tied up."

"Your word doesn't mean anything," Gene said. "Who are you? Who do you work for?"

"You're not in a position to be asking questions."

His friend laughed — it was an evil laugh. "Even if we told you, you wouldn't believe it."

"Well, Gene, it's now time. I want you to use your superintelligence and logically think through the choices and consequences that you now have before you. You need to understand that if you fail to cooperate, you will die."

"And if I do cooperate, I have only your word that I won't die."

"You have a choice between certain death and possible death." He took his pistol and placed it against Gene's temple.

"Shooting me in the head would destroy whatever you want."

The man chuckled. "There are other ways to kill." He placed the gun against Gene's chest. "Better?"

"At least more logical," Gene said.

"What might be even more logical is if we just put an end to this experiment by putting an end to you," he said.

"It will continue without me," Gene said.

"We can set it back seventeen years. By then, the world might come to its senses and realize what a danger you present to mankind. The decision is yours and must be made immediately or —"

"I'll bring you to the lab. I'll show you where the serum is stored."

"I was counting on your intelligence."

He lowered the gun and offered a smile.

"Let's go. I'll take you to the lab."

They helped Gene to his feet — then there was a blur of movement as Gene reached out his arm and knocked the gun away. The men pounced on him, and they were fighting, struggling — he couldn't possibly overcome the two of them! He needed help, and there was only one person who could provide it.

I didn't have time to think. I threw open the closet door and rushed across the room, swinging the field hockey stick as I ran. There was a sickening crack as it struck one of the men in the side of the head. He crumpled, collapsing to the floor like he was dead. Had I killed him?

Gene struggled with the second man. He was bigger, and he was striking at Gene. He seemed to know the same moves as Gene. I swung the stick at him, hitting him in the back. Without looking, he reached out an arm and struck me in the shoulder, sending me sprawling backward, the stick flying out of my hands. Stunned — sitting on my butt — I watched the fight continue. They crashed against the wall and then the dresser. I pulled myself up and grabbed the field hockey stick from where it had fallen.

I raised the stick over my head, ready to swing, but there was no clear opening as they were so close and shifting and spinning — and then I swung. It hit the man solidly at the base of his neck, and he sagged forward ever so slightly. Gene grabbed him and threw him across the room, his body hitting the wall and then falling to the floor.

Gene grabbed the gun from the floor and aimed it at the two men. One was motionless, face down, unmoving, unconscious. The other was down, glaring at us.

"Are you all right?" Gene asked.

"I'm all right. Are you?"

"I'm fine because of you. You should have stayed hidden."

"I didn't think. I just acted. Thank goodness it's over."

The man laughed. "Becky, do you think we're the only agents that were sent?"

"How do you know her name?" Gene asked.

And then I recognized him. "You're the scout from the game."

He laughed. "I was scouting, but it wasn't basketball. And you helped provide some information."

I felt numb.

"Gene, we know everything. We know all about you and your girlfriend. If you'd just come quietly, we would have had no reason to have anything to do with her. But now it's —"

"Shut up or I'll put a bullet between your eyes," Gene snapped.

The man smiled. "Is being homicidal a fault they couldn't eliminate or an intentional feature of your design?"

Gene aimed the gun directly at him.

"Go ahead. Killing me won't save you. Or her. You know the two of us didn't come alone."

"Gene, is he right? Are there others?"

He nodded. "They work in teams."

"Who works in teams? Who are they?" I demanded.

"I don't know for sure. I just know they're professionals, agents, operatives, killers."

"Apparently not professional enough," the man said, chuckling.

Why was he laughing? How could he be joking about any of this?

"How many more of you are there?" Gene asked.

He smirked in answer.

We needed help. I pulled out my phone. There was no signal. I could get reception at the window.

"I can call for help," I said, holding up my phone as if I was showing the evidence.

"Your phone won't work," the man said.

"I assume you're using an electronic jamming device to dampen cell and radio signals," Gene said.

"We have a telecommunications jammer as part of the perimeter guard."

"Becky, you won't be able to make a phone call, but even if you could get through, there's nobody to call."

"We *need* to call the police."

"No, we can't. We can't do that to them. We can't do that to Liv," Gene said.

"What do you mean?"

"It might be her father who responds to the call. The police would be driving into a trap. Whoever is watching the perimeter of the property have bigger guns than the police, are better trained, have surprise on their side, and wouldn't hesitate to simply kill them. We can't draw anybody into this."

"Then what do we do?"

"Gene, if you give up, get me the serum, and leave with me, we'll spare her life," the man said.

Gene didn't answer. Had he said "spare my life"? Was he talking about killing me?

"But then again, you'd only want to save her if you had real emotions, and we both know your *kind* doesn't have emotions."

"Shut up!" Gene yelled.

"Anger is different from emotions. Does she really think you care for her?"

"He loves me!"

"I guess that's possible. People love their pets, and that's basically all you could ever be to his *kind*."

Gene brought the gun up and aimed it directly at the man's face.

"Go ahead. You'd like to kill me, wouldn't you?" the man asked. "It's part of your genetics, isn't it? You might even enjoy it."

"I'm not going to kill you," Gene said. "Unless I have to." He lowered the gun and turned slightly so he could face me.

"Becky, if I could trade my life for your life, I'd do it in a second, but I know that even if I give up, these people aren't going to allow any witnesses. They can't leave you alive to report what happened."

I felt like I'd been punched in the stomach.

"We have an operative on each side of the house," the man said. "There's no way you can leave here without being seen. You're trapped."

But I realized he might be wrong. "How long have you been surrounding the house?" I asked.

"Over three hours. Nobody is getting out, and nobody is getting in to help you."

I turned to Gene. "But they didn't know I was here. They didn't see me come in."

"That's right. You weren't looking for her because you didn't know she was here," Gene said.

"They didn't see me come in, which means they're not going to see us when we leave. Gene, we can escape the same way I got in."

Gene nodded. "But we can't go yet. There are things I have to do first."

21

GENE CHECKED THE ropes that bound the two men. He'd tied them up at the ankles and knees, their hands were bound behind their backs, and they were also tied to the bed frame. I stood awkwardly to the side, holding the pistol. The first man I'd hit on the head was only semiconscious with just the occasional groan or fluttering of his eyes.

Gene checked the ropes and tightened them a little more.

"Tying us up doesn't save you. You got lucky, but even if you get out of the house without being seen, how far do you think you'll get?"

"It's a big world," Gene replied.

"Not so big that we couldn't find you here."

"Big talk from the man who's tied up." Gene turned to me and said, "You should wait here."

"Where are you going?"

"I have to check on my parents. I'll be back soon."

"I have to go with you. Please don't leave me."

He hesitated before answering. "Let me go downstairs first and make sure it's safe. Okay?"

I nodded and offered him the pistol.

"You need to keep it. If he tries to get loose, you need to shoot him."

"What?"

"He's tied up, but just in case. I'll take the second gun."

He went over and picked it up off the window ledge, and then he was gone.

"It's not too late for you to get out of this," the man said. "We don't want you. Only him. Untie me. We'll lock you in the closet and we'll leave."

"I'm not untying you."

"You would if you knew what was really happening here. You have no idea who he is."

"I know exactly who he is."

"You don't even know *what* he is. You think he's human. He's another species."

"Yeah, he's an alien." Had this guy been talking to Liv?

"He's not an alien, but he isn't a human. He's not like you or me."

"I'm nothing like *you*!" I snapped.

Gene came back into the room. "There's nobody else in the house. We're all right to go downstairs."

"She'd be safer here with me," the man said. "At least we're the same species and —"

Gene stuffed a sock in the man's mouth. He then grabbed a shirt and wrapped it around like a gag to stop him from spitting it out.

"We haven't got much time. Come on."

Gene went to the door. With a backward glance at the two men tied to the edge of the bed, I rushed forward to be right by Gene as he started down the stairs. He held his pistol out in front of him. I held mine off to the side.

Getting to the main floor, I saw there was furniture knocked over — then I caught sight of his father. He was sitting on the sofa. His head was slightly back, his eyes were open, and there was a gaping hole in his chest with blood staining everything. I gasped.

"I'm so sorry you had to see this."

"Is he …"

"He's dead."

Those two men tied up in Gene's room had murdered him. I felt completely numb.

Off to the side, I saw a pair of legs sticking out from behind a chair. I knew they belonged to Gene's mother. I gestured.

"I'm so sorry. You've lost your parents."

"I'm sorry they were killed, but they're not my parents. They're members of the team of research scientists who have been part of the project since before I was even born. They were assigned to monitor this aspect of the project."

I tried to process what he'd just said. There was that word, *project*, again. It made no sense. None of this made sense.

Gene punched a code into the keypad on the basement door, and it opened. It was thick metal, like a bank vault door. That was why they couldn't get down there.

"Should I wait up here?" I asked.

"No, I don't want you to be left alone up here, and I need your help to do things as quickly as possible."

I started down the stairs. Gene pulled the door closed with a loud thud, and we were sealed inside. I felt safe and trapped all at once.

I followed him down. It was like I'd stepped inside a laboratory or a hospital. There were stainless steel counters, microscopes and trays, gigantic refrigerators, shelves with tubes and vials, two hospital beds, and, in the corner, the big MRI scanner he'd told me about.

Gene began taking papers out of a filing cabinet and putting them into a briefcase.

"Becky, take all of those scans off the viewer and bring them here."

On the wall were a series of lit boxes — the sort you see in hospital TV shows — and on each of the screens was a brain scan. I was familiar with them because I'd seen the scans of my brain. I put the gun down on the counter and started pulling them off.

I brought them over to Gene, who put them into the briefcase.

Next, he went over to the one of the cupboards. He keyed in a code and opened it up. Inside were vials. He picked up the first two tubes and held them up for me to see.

"Is that the serum?" I asked.

"How do you know about the serum?"

"I heard them asking you about it."

Gene took the two tubes, removed the stoppers, and dumped them down the sink.

"We can't take it all with us, and we can't leave any behind."

He started the tap, and the water washed down what he'd dumped. "Help me."

There were at least two dozen tubes. We each grabbed two. Rushing to the sink, I followed Gene's lead as we dumped the clear liquid into the rushing water and then rinsed out the empty tubes.

"This is what they wanted," I said. "This is what they killed for."

He nodded.

"And you're just destroying it."

"We know the formula. If they had a sample, they could analyze it and then reproduce it."

When there were only four tubes of serum left, Gene said, "These come with us."

Carefully, he placed them in the briefcase. He locked it and then handed it to me. I held on to the handle with one hand and then wrapped my other arm around the case.

Gene reached down and grabbed a backpack and slung it over one shoulder. He took a second identical bag and handed it to me. I slung it over my shoulder. He took the briefcase back and held the pistol in his other hand.

"We have to leave now."

I picked up the second gun from the counter.

We went up the stairs, and once again he sealed the big door to the basement. I tried hard not to look at his parents — at the two bodies that we were leaving behind.

We climbed the stairs and went into his room. The first man I'd hit was now awake but still dazed. The other was still sitting there tied up, but his gag was out, and something seemed wrong. He looked like he was hiding something. I pointed the gun directly at him.

"Raise your hands," I said, looking straight at him.

"That's hard to do with my hands tied behind my back."

"Raise your hands. Now!"

The man smiled and then slowly raised his hands. The tie was attached to only one hand.

"How did you know?" Gene asked me.

"He looked guilty."

"He is guilty. He killed them, and he didn't need to," Gene said. "They weren't a threat to you."

"They wouldn't comply," the man said.

"I should do to you what you did to them."

He laughed. "It sounds like they haven't worked out the homicidal side effects of gene splicing."

What did any of that mean?

"I don't imagine you had any emotional attachment to them, so if you kill me it won't be for revenge."

"It might be about justice, or that you didn't comply," Gene said. His voice was calm and quiet.

The man turned to me. "Do you know what sort of monster you're dealing with?"

"There's only one monster in this room, and it's you!" I snapped.

He laughed. I didn't expect that. "He's Frankenstein. He's not like you or me or anybody else in the world. Do you really think that he cares about *human* life?"

"I don't care about one human's life," Gene said. "If you want to stay alive, you'll tell me how you found us."

He smirked. "Why not? It's not like you're getting away anyway. It's all because you decided you needed to become a basketball star. Your face appeared on basketball websites, Instagram pictures, and your lovely little town newspaper."

"That still doesn't explain how you found us," Gene said.

"Your face popped up in our deep dive of the web with our facial recognition software."

"I don't understand," I said.

"There are special software programs that the government and police forces use," Gene said. "They can scan all pictures on the internet including social media, websites, blogs, and newspapers from around the world and look for facial recognition matches."

"That sounds unbelievable."

"It's a recent development, but that couldn't be it."

"Why not?" I asked.

"They'd need a picture for the match, and there are no pictures of me available for them to compare."

"Not recent pictures," the man said. "The one we were using was almost seven years old. We utilized an aging application. Then again, you'd be surprised how much we know about you. Money and greed can unlock many doors. Would you like to know who sold us the keys to your lock?"

Gene didn't answer.

"I can tell you it all. I know everything. Sit down, and I'll explain everything," he said.

"I know what you're doing," Gene said. "You're trying to keep us here as long as possible. You know the rest of your people are coming into the house, and soon."

I knew they were outside but hadn't thought about them coming in.

"Wherever you go, we'll find you," the man said. He turned to me again. "Becky, we know where you live, where your parents work. You may be standing there with the guns now, but somebody is going to find you, find you both."

"Somebody might find us, but it's not going to be you," Gene said.

Like lightning, he brought the gun down against the side of the man's skull, and there was a sickening thud.

I felt a wave of nausea sweep through my body, and I thought I was going to throw up.

"I'm sorry you had to see that," Gene said.

"Is he … did you … did you kill him?"

"He's alive. I applied enough blunt force to render him unconscious but not enough to fracture his skull. He's going to have a splitting headache when he wakes up."

Gene started going through the man's pockets. He pulled out a wallet and a cellphone. There was a timer on the phone's screen — it showed 3:12 and counting down.

"Why is there a countdown?" I asked.

Gene didn't answer. He was already going through the second man's pockets. Again, he pulled out his wallet and his cellphone. He turned the cellphone so I could see the screen. It was also counting down and was at 2:47.

"The whole team synchronized their phones before these two entered the house. If these two don't come out before the end of the time, then the others will enter."

"Then we have to leave."

"We're going to time it so as they come through the doors, we're going out the window. But I have one more thing I have to do. Can you close the window, please?"

I walked over to follow his direction and stopped. Why did he want me to close the window when that was our way out? I turned around. He was holding a pillow against one of the men's faces and pressing the gun against the pillow.

"What are you doing?" I screamed.

"I'm using the pillow to muffle the sound. I don't want the

gunfire to be heard from outside — that's why I wanted the window closed."

"You're going to kill him?"

"I don't have any choice but to kill them both. They've seen you and know you've seen them. They'll have to neutralize you."

"Neutralize … what does that …" And then it came to me. No witnesses. They'd have to kill me, and now he was going to kill them.

"We can't leave them alive to tell anybody about you," he said.

"They already know about me. Everything about me!"

"They don't know you were here now. They don't know you witnessed all of this. And they won't if I kill these two."

"You don't have to kill them. Once we get away, we can go to the police and tell them what happened, and they'll arrest them and protect us," I said.

"The police can't protect us. The only safe place is the compound where I was raised. That's where I've got to go. They're the only people who can fix all of this."

"But you can't just kill them."

"They were going to kill us. If I don't, then it won't be safe for you to stay behind when I run. They'll come after you."

A chill went through my entire body. "Then don't leave me behind. Take me with you."

"To the compound?"

"To wherever you go. That's where I want to be. Unless you want to leave me behind," I said.

"Thinking about not being with you causes me pain, right here," he said, touching a hand to his chest. "I didn't know what love was, and then I didn't know how much it can hurt." His voice caught over the last few words. "I love you."

"I love you, and that's why you have to take me with you."

"If I kill them, then nobody knows you were here. We'll get out of here, and you can go back home, back to school, back to your family, and you'll be safe."

"Will I? That man said they know everything about me. Not just him, but *them*. What if they still come after me to find out what I know?"

I could tell he was thinking, trying to weigh all the options, figuring out the consequences. This was my life. He knew it, and so did I.

I walked over and took the pillow from him and took his hand in mine.

"No matter what happens, my life will never be the same. Just take me with you," I said.

"It's going to be dangerous."

"More dangerous than leaving me behind?"

He shook his head. "I don't know."

"Then you have no choice."

The alarms on the phones went off, and I jumped. They were going to come in!

"Okay," Gene said. "Time for us to leave."

22

I LOOKED UP at Gene in the branches above my head as he pushed the window closed. He didn't want to leave a trail to show how we might have escaped. He was holding the briefcase, and we were each wearing one of the backpacks. We moved down from branch to branch. I was trying to focus on the task at hand, working hard not to think of anything else — not the bodies, not the men we'd left behind, not that Gene had been going to kill them, and certainly not the others who were coming to kill us. Were those other men already inside the house and starting to search?

I got to the bottom branch, hesitated for a second, and then dropped to the ground, into the open. I crouched down, staying close, hoping the trunk would hide me. Anxiously, eyes wide open, ears perked, I looked and listened. There was nothing to see or hear. Gene dropped down gently beside me. He pulled the pistol out of his waistband.

"Lead us out the way you came in," Gene whispered.

Crossing the open space, I felt so exposed. I pictured some-body rounding the corner of the house, pulling a weapon, and firing at us. We reached the side of the garage and disappeared from view. Safer, but far from safe. We hurried along the length of the building and disappeared into the weeds. I tried to stay low, occasionally peering behind me to see Gene doing the same.

We quickly arrived at the fence and then at the gap. I dropped to my belly and started to climb underneath but was caught. The pack on my back was hooked on the bottom strand of wire.

"Here, let me help you," Gene offered. He unhooked the wire, and I popped out the other side.

Gene had removed his bag and fed it, and then the briefcase, under the fence. He crawled through the gap and then jumped to his feet. I led us into the corn.

"You need to control your breathing," he said.

I realized that I was almost gasping for air. I was also shaking, trembling. My thoughts were racing, and I could feel my pulse, the blood coursing through my chest and in my ears.

"I think I'm going to vomit."

"You're feeling the adrenaline rush starting to subside. The corn is sheltering us — just sit." He offered me a hand, and I lowered myself to the ground. He sat beside me.

He pulled the pack off his back. He rummaged around and pulled out a bottle. "Drink this. It tastes like water, but it's a mixture that's infused with vitamins, minerals, and caffeine."

"Caffeine, like coffee?"

"More like a hyperconcentrated espresso. Caffeine increases brain functioning, reduces muscle fatigue, and retards hunger."

I took a sip. It did taste like water. I took a much deeper drink.

"Are these bags like tornado escape kits?" I asked. "We have three of them in our basement."

"They are escape kits, but not for a tornado." I waited for him to elaborate, but he didn't.

Gene pulled out the wallets he'd taken from the two men. They were identical black leather. He started to go through one. He pulled out pieces of identification.

"Who is he?"

"According to his driver's license his name is John Brown." He showed me the ID, and the picture was of the man whom he'd gagged — the one who had been talking to me, the one who'd pretended to be a scout.

"I didn't know who he was back in the gym or I wouldn't have talked to him."

"You would have had no way of knowing," Gene said.

"But I told him things about you!"

"You didn't tell him anything he didn't already know or he wouldn't have been there to begin with. It's not your fault."

That made me feel better even if it wasn't true. "Who is he?"

"He lives at 789 Eighth Avenue, New York, New York, but that wouldn't be his real address or his real name. He also has a library card, health provider card, and three credit cards in that name."

Gene pulled out a wad of bills — they all looked like crisp, new twenty-dollar bills — and some receipts. As he unfolded the receipts, I looked. They were from a hardware store, a grocery store, and a bookstore. Each had a prominent New York City address at the very top.

"He's definitely from New York," I said.

"Not necessarily."

He dropped the wallet, ID, and money to the ground and opened up the second wallet. He went through it. This driver's license showed a photo of the first man I'd hit with the stick. Aside

from a different name and address — he lived in Chicago —
he had the exact same pieces of ID, wad of new bills, and three
receipts from three different stores in Chicago — one a hardware
store, the second a grocery store, and the third a bookstore.

"These are cover identification provided by whoever they
work for."

"Who *do* they work for?"

"I don't know. It could be a private company or a foreign
government or —"

"Do you mean they could be spies?"

"Agents of some kind."

"But they didn't speak with any accent."

"They could be double agents or sleepers, or even members
or former members of one of our own government agencies."

"It can't be that. Our government doesn't just go and kill
people," I said.

He didn't answer. Instead, he asked a question. "If we go
through this field in the direction we're heading, where does it
take us?"

"Out to Elm Street. If we get out there, we can still get to the
police station and get help. We could even call them."

I pulled out my phone. There was a signal!

He put his hand on my hand. "You can't do that. The way they
were able to block cellphones means that they'll also be monitoring all calls. In fact, they'll be able to triangulate your signal
from the cell tower where your phone pings, and they'll know
exactly where we are."

"They can do that?" I asked.

"That technology is more than a decade old."

"But we have to let the police know. We need their help."

"Even if we got in touch with the police, even if they believed us —"

"Why wouldn't they believe us?" I demanded.

"You were there. You saw it all happen. Does it sound believable to you?"

Of course it didn't.

"Even then, it still wouldn't be safe. Nobody will be safe, not even the police."

"But they're the *police*. They have guns."

"The people who are pursuing us will have bigger guns and more men."

"But there's only six of them, and two are injured. The Nobleton police department is five times that big."

"Once they find I've slipped away, the area will be flooded with operatives. They'll come and kill anybody who gets in the way. I'm so sorry for getting you into this."

"It's not your fault, but I still need to make at least one phone call … to my parents. Is that all right?"

"It has to be short. We can't risk them finding us, and you really can't tell them anything or it puts them at risk."

"Do you mean they could harm my parents?"

He shook his head. "They want your parents alive in case you come back or send for them. As long as your parents know nothing, they're safe."

I felt a rush of relief.

"Becky, you've seen what they're capable of doing, so we need to protect your parents by staying away. The call has to be short. Less than thirty seconds."

"But what would I say to them? How can I explain this to my mother, to my father?"

"You can't. Tell them you can't come home. Tell them you had to run away."

"How soon will I be able to call them again? How soon will I be able to go home?"

"I'm not sure. It could be a few days. It could be longer."

I took the phone and called my mother's cell. It rang once, then twice, then three times. Why wasn't she picking up?

"I think it's going to voice mail," I said to Gene. "I'll call my father or —"

"No, you can't. One call. Leave a message."

"I can't just leave a message."

"There's no choice."

And there was no time to argue. The message started to play.

"I'm not available. Leave a message and I'll get back to you as soon as possible." Her voice was so happy and warm and sweet. There was a beep.

"Mom, I love you. I'm so sorry. Something happened. I can't come home right now. It'll be days before you hear from me again. I'm fine. Gene is with me. He's going to keep me safe. There was no choice. We had to run. I love you and Dad so much. Goodbye."

I hung up and started to cry, and Gene wrapped his arms around me. There were tears in his eyes too.

23

"YOU NEED TO turn your phone off now," Gene said.

"I won't use it."

"It doesn't matter if it's being used. Your phone is in continuous communication with the cell towers. A signal goes back and forth updating your apps, texts, and data. If somebody knows your number, they can access that data and discover which cell towers your phone is pinging off. The direction of movement can be mapped and your location discovered."

"I didn't know that."

"In fact, your phone's microphone and camera can be remotely turned on so what you're saying and what you're seeing can be monitored and recorded. It's done all the time."

"But those men can't do that, can they?"

"If they could find me to begin with and can jam telecommunications networks, then I'm sure they can track us through our phones. I'm also concerned that within a few hours they'll even be able to utilize satellite imagery to track us."

"Now I'm even more lost."

"There are keyhole satellites that are equipped with high-resolution cameras that are so powerful they can read the numbers on a license plate, so they're capable of seeing us."

I looked up at the clear blue sky. "But only governments have satellites."

"Private companies have satellites, but what if this is a foreign government that we're running from? What if it's a branch of our government with satellite access?"

"I still don't believe it could be our government."

"It makes more sense if it is. It would explain why they knew so much about the project."

Somehow that did make frightening sense — frightening that it could be our government, and frightening that they might be behind killing two innocent people.

"I know it sounds like fantasy, but you have to believe me," Gene said.

"The strangest thing is that I *do* believe you." I turned off my phone.

"Let's put your phone inside of your bag," he said, holding open the backpack.

I dropped it in.

"These packs are specially designed. They have lead linings that dampen any signal transmission."

"But if the phone is turned off that shouldn't be a problem, should it?"

"I'm not certain that there's not a further internal tracking system embedded in phones that allows remote tracking that I'm not aware of."

"That's just being paranoid," I said.

"There are so many levels of things going on that nobody's aware of. Think about what just happened."

With his pack still open, he removed the gun from his belt, and I took the second out of my pocket. We placed them both inside, and he zipped it up once more.

"I'm assuming they've untied and revived their operatives and know that you're with me and that we're gone. We have to get more distance between us and them. To the right is the town. What's in the other direction?"

I had to think about it. "This is the McGregor farm. It goes on forever. It's probably four hundred acres of corn."

"And beyond that?"

"More corn and then more corn. Sometimes it seems like Indiana is nothing but corn."

"Let's stay in the corn."

"Wait, shouldn't we at least take the money?"

The ground was littered with the ID and money from the two wallets.

"Their money could be tagged with microprocessors to reveal location. Besides, each of these packs contain twenty-five thousand dollars in cash. It's in small bills, twenties and tens. Untraceable."

"I don't think I've ever seen that much money in one place," I said.

"Neither have I. Actually, before moving to Nobleton I'd never seen money at all."

"That can't be true."

"I was raised in a compound. Everything I needed was provided. When you and Liv brought me to buy clothes, that was the first store I'd ever been inside."

That made no sense and complete sense all at once. There were so many things that he had never done before, so many experiences that were new to him.

I looked at him. I looked into his eyes. He saw me staring, and he smiled. The same gentle smile I'd seen that first time in the guidance office. He reached out and took my hand, and I felt a little jolt of electricity. He was so very different from anybody else I'd ever known.

And then I thought about what that agent had said — about him being a different species. That was so ridiculous. It was all so ridiculous. It seemed more like a novel or a spy movie. The problem was that I couldn't put the book down or walk out of the movie theater. This was real, and it was happening to me.

WE MOVED ROW by row through the corn. I kept looking up for the unseen satellite in the sky and then glancing back and listening for anybody coming from behind. The only sound was the wind rustling through the cornstalks. The only sight was the blue sky and a few puffy white clouds. The sun had gotten so low that it was hidden behind the stalks. We were walking through the shadows, and it was starting to get cold.

I kept thinking about the scene in the house. I couldn't get that man's face out of my mind or his voice out of my ears. And there were the bodies. Two dead bodies. I'd seen dead people before. That was part of volunteering at a seniors' residence. What wasn't part of it was seeing people who'd been murdered. I just wished I could talk to my parents about what had happened. They'd heard my message by now and had probably tried to call me a thousand times. They must be worried to death. If only I could give them a call.

Gene was walking ahead of me. In his right hand was the briefcase with all the information. And the vials of liquid — the serum. I hadn't even thought about that until now.

"The serum, what is it?" I asked.

"It's a part of the program. It's the culmination of decades of research, the product of the life work of countless scientists and researchers."

"So, it's worth millions of dollars," I said.

"Not millions. *Billions*. No, that's wrong. It's priceless, and that's why I couldn't risk it falling into the wrong hands."

"But why didn't you pour *all* of it away?" I asked.

"I thought it might be needed in our escape. You have to make me a promise," Gene said. "If something happens to me, if my functioning is compromised or I'm killed."

A chill went up my spine. "If they'd kill you, does that mean they'd kill me?"

He didn't answer, but of course I already knew.

"If that happens, and you're able, you have to promise that you'll destroy the remaining vials. You can't let them fall into the wrong hands."

Numbly, I nodded my head. "Is this stuff what makes you smart?"

He didn't answer. He looked like he was thinking it through, weighing the variables. Finally, he spoke. "My intelligence is based on a variety of elements, and this serum is one of the major components. It's an enzyme. What do you know about babies?"

"They're cute, they sleep a lot, they wear diapers."

"And they learn quickly. Think about how they acquire information like language."

"I don't know if it's that quickly; it takes years for a child to learn to talk," I said.

"Language is only part of the huge passive learning that they absorb."

"I don't know what 'passive learning' means."

"When you're studying for a test or trying to learn anything new, you have to *actively*, consciously, systematically try to input, integrate, and then utilize that information. If you were to try to learn to speak French now, you'd have to actively try to learn."

"And babies don't need to study to do that," I said.

"No. Information just naturally enters their minds because of brain-derived neurotropic factor, or BDNF for short."

"And the stuff in those vials, that's the enzyme."

"It's a synthesized, much more concentrated version of that enzyme. Not only is passive learning enabled, but it happens so much faster."

"How much faster?"

Gene didn't answer. He tilted his head to the side. It looked like he was listening for something, and then I heard it — a motor. It got louder and louder. There was a flash of red in the gap of blue between the cornstalks, and a small plane roared over top of us. The sound of the engine got quieter with each passing second until it died away completely.

"I'm sure nobody could have seen us," Gene said, "but why would a plane be here?"

"There's a small airport south of here."

"How far south?" Gene asked.

I shrugged. "I'm not sure, but I think about thirty miles."

"We need to get there, but not tonight. It's going to get dark soon. We have to find a place under cover. I want a roof over our heads to hide our heat patterns."

"You're going to explain that, right?"

"All living creatures emit heat. A satellite or an airplane or even a drone equipped with thermography — thermal imaging — can see the heat patterns of living things."

"Couldn't they see us now?"

"During the day, the sun heats up everything so our heat signature is lost in a sea of warmth. At night, as it cools, we become more visible. We glow red on the monitor, and the background is blue or green."

"It isn't like there are a lot of options out here."

"We'll find something." Gene looked at his watch. "And hopefully within ninety minutes."

24

I OPENED MY eyes. It was dark, but there were little leaks of light coming through the cracks and holes in the shed. It wasn't morning yet, but it wasn't night either. As my eyes adjusted, I could see the farm tools hanging on the walls and the tractor in the corner. What I couldn't see was Gene.

I pushed off the crinkly metal space blanket. Gene's blanket was off to the side. These blankets were thin, but mine had kept me amazingly warm. Well, the combination of that and being fully dressed.

Just before dark, we'd come out of the corn and stumbled on to a farm lane. We'd trailed along it until we found their drive shed. I'd thought there was no way that, lying in the dirt with so many questions percolating in my mind, I'd be able to sleep. Instead, the moment my head hit the ground I was out like a light. Now that I was awake, those thoughts came rushing back again.

My parents must be going crazy. What would they be thinking? I was sure the first place my father would have gone was Gene's house. Was he the one who'd discovered the bodies, or had he found the police already there? I shuddered at the thought. What would he think had happened? What would *everybody* think?

I got up and moved toward the door. Gene had probably gone out and looked around or — a terrible thought entered my mind.

He'd left me here and just gone off on his own. Then I saw the briefcase sitting just off to the side. He'd never have left that briefcase. He'd never leave me, either.

There was a creak, and the door opened and Gene appeared.

"Good morning," I said. "Have you been up for a while?"

"I went out to do some scouting."

"And?"

"There's a paved highway about one hundred yards in one direction and a farm about the same distance in the other. We need to get a ride or find a car that we can take."

"Then I think we should go to the farmhouse. We can tell them our car has broken down and ask if it's possible for them to give us a ride to the airport."

"Do you think they'll do it?"

"Of course they will. This is Indiana. But if they don't volunteer a ride, we can also offer them some money. We certainly have enough of that."

"That makes sense. Let's go."

JUST BEFORE WE left the shed, we heard a vehicle coming. We peeked through a gap and saw a blue pickup truck drive past, leaving a trail of dust behind it. We might have missed our chance to get a ride, but luckily, we hadn't been discovered coming out of their drive shed.

The farmhouse was a big, rambling three-story building with a porch that wrapped around three sides. Sitting by the barn was an old pickup truck and an even older car. Both were covered in dust and dirt the way all farm vehicles seemed to be.

"Do you think anybody's home?" Gene asked.

"Even if there isn't anybody here, I bet the keys are in the car and the truck. Let me do the talking."

As we stepped onto the porch, we heard a dog barking, and then a big hound came charging around the corner of the house. It was still barking like crazy, but it was also wagging its tail.

I bent down. "Good boy," I said as I gave him a rub behind the ears. "You're just doing your job, aren't you? Although you have to stop wagging your tail if you want to look scary."

I heard the door open and looked up. A woman about my mother's age had come out. She was in jeans and a checkered shirt. She offered a big smile and a greeting.

"Good morning," she sang out.

"Good morning," I replied as I stood up.

"Sorry to trouble you, especially this early," Gene said.

"It's a farm, so we've been up for …" She stopped mid-sentence. She looked at Gene, then at me, and her expression suddenly changed. Her smile faded and was replaced by a look of confusion, then disbelief, and finally terror. And then she bolted.

She ran a few steps toward the door, threw open the screen, ran inside, and went to slam the door closed. Gene put his shoulder against the door, bumping it open, and went into the house. I ran in after him. The woman was on the floor, and Gene was standing over her holding a shotgun.

"What are you doing?" I demanded.

Gene didn't answer.

"Are you all right?" I asked as I offered the woman a hand and helped her to her feet.

She brushed my hand aside and scurried slightly backward on her bottom. She looked terrified. "Please don't hurt me!"

I was too shocked to understand, but Gene was holding a shot-gun. Where had that gun come from?

"We're not going to hurt you," I assured her. "Our car broke down on the highway and …" I realized there was no point in trying out our story with Gene standing there holding a weapon.

"Gene, where did you get the shotgun?"

"I took it from her. She ran back in here to get it."

I turned to the woman. "But why did you think you needed a gun?"

She didn't answer, but she didn't look any less afraid.

"Gene, for goodness' sake, put down the gun."

"Not yet." He turned to the woman. "Who else is in the house?"

She shook her head. "Nobody else … please, don't hurt me."

"Gene, put down the gun, please, you're scaring her, and me."

He lowered it. "Who was in that truck that drove away?"

She didn't answer.

"Tell me!" Gene yelled threateningly.

"It was my husband and our kids. He was driving them to school."

"When will he be back?" Gene demanded.

"Not till late this afternoon. He's got errands to run in town, and then he'll just wait around and drive them back after school is over."

Gene put the shotgun down, propping it against the wall and tucking it behind the door. The woman looked relieved but still scared. I felt the same.

"I won't tell anybody you were here. Please, just leave. I'm a mother, think of my children." She burst into tears.

"I promise, we're not going to hurt you. Please believe me," I said.

She didn't answer. The only sound was coming from a television in another room.

"Do those vehicles work?" Gene asked.

"Yes, both of them. The keys are in the ignition. You can tie me up so I won't be able to contact anybody until you're long gone." She started crying louder, sobbing.

I bent down and wrapped my arms around her. She was shaking badly.

"Please, tell me, tell us, why did you think you needed to get the gun? Why do you think we might hurt you?"

She sobbed and said only two words: "The TV."

"The TV?" I looked at Gene. He picked the shotgun back up and went into the other room. I helped her to her feet and, with my arm still around her, guided her into the room.

It was tuned to CNN. There were two reporters talking, and I skidded to a stop. Behind them were pictures of me and Gene.

"Gene, it's us."

"As the victims died of gunshot wounds and no weapons have been found, we have to assume that the two young suspects are still armed and dangerous," the male reporter said.

"While the police have only announced that the young couple are people of interest, my sources have confirmed that they are suspected to be the killers. If you see them, please do not approach. Contact the police immediately," the female reporter added.

It felt like I'd been kicked in the stomach. How could they think that we'd killed Gene's parents? We weren't the people who'd done this, we were running from them!

The backdrop changed to a picture of Gene's house. There were police cars in the driveway, lights flashing.

"It is possible that the girl, identified as Becky James, has simply been taken hostage," the female reporter said.

My mouth dropped open.

"Sources have also shared that the young man may have a history of violent behavior. It is believed these actions happened prior to his sixteenth birthday, so his record is sealed as a minor. Reports are surfacing that he has previously —"

Gene clicked the television off.

"Gene, how could they think that we did this?" I turned directly to the woman. "We would never do any of that. We're innocent! You have to believe me!"

She didn't look convinced, only more scared.

"Do you have rope?" he asked the woman.

She didn't answer.

"We can tie you up or kill you, it's your choice," he said to her.

"Gene, what are you saying?"

"Shut up!" he yelled at me. "I've had enough of you as well. You're lucky I took you hostage instead of killing you!"

What was he saying? What did he mean?

"Do you have any rope?" he asked again.

"In the back room," she said.

"Go and get it," he yelled at me. "And don't even think about trying to escape!"

I stumbled out of the room. My mind spun around, searching for meaning. Why was he saying these things? Gene had never yelled at me or … And then it came to me. This was a performance. If the woman saw me as having been taken hostage, then she, and anyone she talked to, would believe I wasn't involved in any of this. I was innocent. I wasn't a killer. Gene had put it all on him. He was putting on a show to protect me.

The back room was filled with horse riding tack — saddles and reins and bridles — and I saw the rope. I picked up a couple loops of rope and returned to find the woman sitting on a kitchen chair.

"Tie her up," Gene ordered.

I walked over and placed a hand on her shoulder. "I'm so sorry," I said quietly. "Please let me know if it's too tight or if it hurts."

I looped the first piece of rope around the spindles of the chair and then around her wrists. I tied them, trying to be careful but making sure the rope was still tight enough to hold her in place.

"Is that all right?" I asked, and she nodded.

I circled around, took another piece of rope, and tied it around the chair legs and her legs. I was finished.

"Now you sit down in the chair beside her," he said.

"What?"

"Sit down while I decide whether I'm going to take you with me or tie you up as well."

"You can't do that."

"Sit down!" he ordered.

I sat down. Gene began pacing the room. He looked like he was thinking.

"Get up," he ordered. "You're coming with me. I still need a hostage."

Gene turned to the woman. "When did you last have something to eat?"

She looked confused but answered. "Breakfast, I had breakfast an hour ago."

"Get her water, and some food. She could be here for hours before somebody comes."

I went into the kitchen and realized that Gene had followed me.

"Sorry, I couldn't warn you," he whispered. "I did this for the news, for your parents. I want them to know you weren't involved."

"I understand, I guess. You weren't really going to leave me, were you?"

"If I thought you were safe, I would have left you at the house to begin with. As soon as I didn't kill those two men, it was never safe to leave you."

"But why do the police think we killed your parents?"

"What else would they think? They found the bodies of my parents, and we've run away. We sure look guilty. Besides, somebody is trying to control the narrative. Probably the same people, the same organization, we're running from. By making us fugitives, they get every police officer in the country looking for us."

"We need to call the police to let them know the truth."

"We can't call anybody. They'll trace our location."

"Couldn't we just turn ourselves in and explain it all?" I asked.

"If we're taken prisoner by the police, there won't be time for us to explain anything. Those men and others like them will storm the station, kill the police, capture us, and even make it look like we were the ones who killed the police in our escape."

"But they're the police. They can protect us and themselves."

He put his hands on my shoulders. "No, they can't. You saw

what these people are capable of. The compound is the only place where we'll be safe. It's our only chance." He paused. "Do you believe me?"

I nodded.

"Can you please grab one of those bottles of water and one of those bananas? It's going to be a long day for her. I feel bad, but there's nothing else we can do."

I gathered the items, and Gene went over to the counter and yanked the phone out of the wall jack and then, with his foot, knocked the jack completely off the wall.

"I want you to write a letter to your parents," he said. He'd picked up a pad of paper. "We're going to leave it here. Try to reassure them, tell them that I've taken you hostage."

"But that makes you look like a murderer, a kidnapper. Why can't I just tell them the truth?"

"They wouldn't believe you if you did. It just puts them in danger. You have to remember this letter is going to be read by more than just your parents. The police and the FBI will read it. It will hit the press and make its way to CNN and beyond."

"I'd rather write nothing than lie about you, about the situation."

"Becky, I feel so awful for all of this, for putting your life at risk. The least I need to do is give you a way back from all of this, a way to regain your life."

"But what about you?"

"My life isn't my own. It never has been. Please, just write the letter. We have to leave. Quickly."

I nodded. "I'll do it. I just have to figure out what to write."

25

THE LETTER WAS hard to write. I stopped half a dozen times, unsure what to say. I gave the woman — it turned out her name was Janice — swigs of water and had her eat the banana between the words I was writing.

She and I talked, and I tried to reassure her that she was going to be okay. She now thought I was in just as much danger as she was. Gene's acting job had worked. At one point, as Gene left the house, she asked me to just run out the back door into the corn, disappear, and escape. Despite all that was happening to her, she was worried about me. I told her there wasn't time for me to untie her, and I wasn't leaving without her.

I signed the letter. It felt good to say something to my parents, but wrong to say so little and to deceive them in what I was saying.

Gene came back into the room. He'd been out looking at the vehicles and loading our things.

"Are you ready to go?" he asked.

"I just finished the letter."

"Read it to me," he said.

"Sure. 'Dear Mom and Dad. I'm fine. Gene isn't going to hurt me. He would never do that. Things aren't the way they seem. You have to know that I'd never do anything to hurt anybody. I'm not that sort of person. You didn't raise me that way.'"

I felt a catch in my throat. I was close to tears.

"Please," Gene said. "Can you go on? I know it's hard."

I nodded. "'I wish I could just be home. I wish that nothing had happened and I was in school today with Gene in the desk beside me. I know how hard this must be for you, but you have to know that I'll be home soon. I don't know when, but it will happen. It might be a few days, but I'm going to give you the biggest and longest hug I've ever given you. I love you so much. Becky.' Is that all right?"

"That's good." He walked over to Janice. "We're taking the pickup truck. You won't see it again, and I feel bad. It's an old truck. I think it's worth less than two thousand dollars. I've left money — four thousand dollars — on the table so you can replace it."

"But … but why are you doing that?" she asked.

"It wouldn't be fair for your family to lose a truck. Are the ropes all right? They're not too tight?"

"They're fine."

"I had to go through your purse. I took your phone and removed the battery. I also took the battery from the car we're leaving behind. You can buy batteries for both, but I couldn't risk you getting free to make a call or drive to get help or alert the authorities. Are you sure your husband will be back this afternoon?"

"I'm sure."

"Good. It's bad enough to be tied up for the day. I wouldn't want it to be any longer. I think you should probably be able to work yourself free before that. You didn't deserve this," Gene said.

"You could leave her here," Janice said. "She'd soon be with her parents. I know you don't want to hurt her."

"He won't hurt me," I said.

"And I can't leave her. But we have to go," Gene said.

Gene left, and I hesitated at the doorway. I looked at Janice. I wanted to say something, but I just wasn't sure what to say.

"I'll be praying for you," she said. "And if you have a chance, get away, escape."

"He's not going to hurt me. He loves me."

"I know he loves you, and that's the problem. If people are afraid to lose love, they're capable of doing terrible things to keep it. They're capable of anything."

"I'll be fine. I'm so sorry for all of this. So is Gene."

I rushed away, closing the door behind me. Gene was already in the truck, the engine running. He was in the passenger seat. Obviously, he wanted me to drive. I climbed in behind the wheel. The briefcase and the two backpacks were on the floor.

"You can drive standard, right?" he asked.

"I can." I put the truck into first gear, and we started off, away from the farmhouse, down the bumpy laneway, and past the drive shed where we'd spent the night.

"Am I driving because you don't know how to drive a stick?" I asked.

"I have the theoretical knowledge of how to drive, but I've never driven before."

"Never?"

"Of course, if I wanted to drive —"

"You could drive an Indy car and win the Indianapolis 500," I said, cutting him off.

He held out an old, battered, dirty baseball cap. He snugged it into place on my head.

"I thought it would make a good disguise."

"How about you?" I asked.

"I'm just going to stay low. They're looking for two people, so it's best if only one person can be seen in the truck."

We came up to the main road, and Gene slid onto the floor so even the top of his head wasn't visible to anybody looking into the truck. Not that there was anybody to look; the road was deserted as far as I could see in either direction.

"That was a nice letter you wrote your parents."

"I wish I could have told them the truth."

"Telling the truth would have put them in danger. They're safe."

That thought was reassuring. My parents were safe. And Gene's parents were dead.

"Your parents, your adoptive parents, I mean those scientists, you were close to them, right?"

"I probably knew them as well as I knew anybody else in the project."

"But there must have been a strong connection since they were chosen to come with you and pretend to be your parents."

"Their expertise was the best match for that phase of the project. Or at least how the project was originally conceived." His voice cracked over the last few words.

I looked over. A tear was running down his cheek.

"It's okay," I said.

"I know. I'm fine." He tried to snuffle back the tears. "I'm just surprised to be crying."

"It's okay to be upset. They were like family."

"Not family."

"People who've been there from the beginning of your whole life makes them like family," I argued.

"It's different. I wasn't a member of their family. I was their *project*."

"No," I said. "I saw the way they treated you, the way they acted around you. They were proud of you."

Gene started to sob. I was shocked. It was loud and raw. I reached out and put my hand on his shoulder.

"I understand," I said. "It's okay … it's okay."

There was nothing else I could say. I left my hand on his shoulder to let him know I was there. Slowly, his tears started to subside.

"It's just so much more painful than I ever thought it would be," he said through some sniffles. "It's the first time I've lost somebody."

"Really?"

"We have a core group who've been there forever, from the beginning. Nobody has ever left the project."

"Then it's understandable that you're feeling so upset."

"It's more than just upset," he said. "When I came back up to the bedroom, back to those two men, I was so angry."

"You seemed so calm."

"I was calm, but I was also filled with rage. He was right about one thing. I wanted more than anything to kill them, to get revenge."

"I get that too."

"You don't understand," he said. "I've been programmed to be nonviolent."

"Programmed?" I asked.

"I've been trained, educated, indoctrinated to respect all life. It's why I'm a vegetarian. I don't see myself as above other animals. I believe all life is precious."

"That's good."

"Revenge is such a strange, raw emotion. I've never felt it before. Funny, it was the exact opposite of what I feel toward you, but they could both end the same way."

"I don't understand."

"I would kill to protect you." He paused. "I just hope it won't be necessary."

A truck was coming toward us, and I had a sense of apprehension. As it got closer, I realized it was almost as old and beaten up as the one we were driving. Just as it went to pass, the driver raised a hand in greeting, and I did the same.

"They were good people, but I didn't love them. I've never loved anybody until I met you," Gene said.

It still took my breath away to hear him say that.

"And I know nobody has ever loved me before," he continued.

That made me so sad.

"Everything in my life is an experiment. *I* am nothing more than an experiment."

"You're so much more. I'm so lucky that I met you, so lucky that of all the places in the world you showed up in my town, in my school, and in my life."

"There are things I need to tell you, to explain to you."

I went to respond when I caught sight of something in the rear-view mirror. It was coming up quickly. It was a police car!

I instinctively looked at the speedometer. I wasn't speeding, but it could be more than just my speed the cop was interested in. What if Janice had gotten loose and phoned in the description and license plate of the truck?

"Stay down," I said. "There's a police car coming up behind us."

Gene slumped farther down. "Does he have his lights on?"

"No cherry lights." I pulled the baseball cap down as well, trying to hide beneath the shadow of the bill.

The car was coming up fast. I deliberately slowed down. He got closer and closer and then swung out into the empty oncoming lane and raced by us. He hadn't even looked over. I felt a wave of relief wash over me.

26

WE DROVE BY the airport. It was a small private field with what looked like one runway, a dozen hangars, a control tower, a small restaurant, and planes parked all along the runway. We were going to take a plane. I wasn't surprised that Gene knew how to fly. What couldn't he do? At the gate to the airport there was a sign showing the hours of operation. It was open from 6:00 a.m. to 6:00 p.m. every day. We had to wait until everybody had gone home. That was still hours away.

That gave us time to ditch the truck, so we left the airport and found a place to pull off the road and into a big cornfield. The tall rows on each side provided cover in two directions, and the field in front went on forever. I drove as far as I could before getting stuck. We got out.

"We need to cover up our path," Gene said. "We want it to be invisible from all sides, including the air."

Gene walked away and then came back with an armful of stalks from another row and placed them on the hood of the truck. Together we began gathering more stalks from rows farther away. We laid them out on the roof of the truck and put some on the tailgate. We also threw dirt on the vehicle so it was even more camouflaged.

"I think that we should go now," Gene said. "We have to get to the airport. Let's get moving."

We started walking through the field, cutting between the rows of corn. I felt safe, hidden on all sides, but I knew I still wasn't hidden from the sky. Were there eyes up there looking for us, or was Gene just being paranoid? Maybe nobody was looking for us — nobody but the police. He was a fugitive accused of a double murder and kidnapping, and I — we hoped — was believed to be his hostage.

"It's amazing that you can fly a plane."

"I'll get you safely up and, more importantly, safely back down."

"I'm not sure why we didn't just wait in the truck until the airport closes."

"There are some things I have to do before we can fly, so I need to sneak in under the wire."

"And what will I do?"

"Wait outside the fence. Take care of our bags and the briefcase."

"And the serum?"

"Especially the serum."

We caught sight of the control tower over the top of the rows of corn. When we got to the last row, Gene dropped to the ground, and I did the same. The airport was behind a high metal fence, topped with strands of outward-leaning barbed wire. The place already looked deserted.

Two men came out the back door of one of the buildings. There was some writing on the wall, but the letters were too small and faded to read. One of the men was older than the other; he walked with a limp and was wearing a cowboy hat. They walked over to one of the planes. The plane had a single engine and was the same shade of blue as the truck we'd stolen. The older man checked out the wings and kicked the tires as the two men circled around the plane.

"He's doing a preflight inspection," Gene explained.

He finished the check, and they climbed into the plane. The engine started, and even from this distance it was loud. They taxied to the end of the runway and then raced back again, taking off and flying away.

"I better get going now. This might be the best chance," Gene said.

He got to his feet, and I scrambled to get up as well. "Wouldn't it be better to wait until the airport is closed?"

"There are things I need to investigate. I'll be as quick as I can, but it depends on what I find and who I have to hide from."

"Be careful, please."

"I will. Stay low and hidden. And remember, no matter what happens, nobody can get the serum."

"It'll be safe with me."

"I know. I trust you with it. I trust you with my life. I love you."

"I love you."

He leaned over, and we kissed. It was long and warm and sent chills throughout my body.

"I don't want to leave you," he said.

"I'll stay right here."

"No, I mean ever. I want to be with you forever."

"Maybe you should go to Indiana State with me," I suggested.

"I wish we could just rewind a few days. The last eight weeks have been the happiest time of my life."

"Mine too."

"Really?" he asked.

I wrapped my arms around him, squeezing him as tight as I could. I released him. "Now, you'd better get going."

Crouched over, Gene made his way to the fence. Earlier, he'd found a spot by a drainage ditch where water had eroded away a section. He dropped down and disappeared, and within a few seconds he appeared on the other side of the fence. He was moving so casually that anybody watching would think he belonged there.

He walked directly to the building where the men had come from. He opened the door, stepped in, and was gone. I felt relieved, but also more anxious.

Now there was nothing to do but wait. And guard the briefcase. I reached out and pulled it closer. I was hungry and thirsty. We were running low on the special water and had eaten into our food supplies, but there was still some of both left.

I opened up one of the packs and saw the revolvers. I'd opened the one Gene had been carrying. I reached in and very carefully removed one of the pistols. I turned it around, carefully looking at it. It was warm to the touch, black, sleek, smooth, and deadly. Had it been this gun that killed Gene's parents? Was this the gun that would have killed me? I went to put it back in the pack and stopped myself. If I was responsible for the serum, I needed to have some way of defending it. I put the gun on the ground beside the briefcase.

I reached back in and pulled out a half-filled bottle of the special water and an energy bar. I ripped the package open with my teeth and took a big bite. It was amazing how good everything tasted when you were hungry enough.

I thought about where I would be today if I wasn't hiding in this field. Right about now I'd be sitting in the gym bleachers, taking notes, talking to the coaches and watching Gene and the other guys practicing.

Instead, my boyfriend had just gone under the fence at an airport because we were going to steal a plane. We were being chased by mysterious, murderous agents, as well as the police and possibly the FBI. As far as the world knew, I was either a murderer or a hostage who had been kidnapped by a murderer. I'd been there when a murder — no, *two* murders — had taken place; I'd smacked two guys with a field hockey stick, knocking one of them semiconscious. We'd stolen a truck and tied up an innocent woman. Our lives were in danger, and I didn't really know how we could escape and what was going to happen. So much for my SATs being my biggest worry.

My life had been completely torn apart. All of this had happened because of the serum. If only it hadn't been invented or discovered or synthesized or whatever had been done to make it. But then, without it would the project have even existed? Would Gene have needed someone to show him around school? Would I have even met Gene? Would I have fallen in love? Would he be the same person I was in love with? How much of who he was was because of the serum?

In a flash, I knew what I wanted to do. I needed to have a closer look at this thing that had changed my life, that was so valuable it was worth killing for.

I clicked the locks and opened the briefcase. There were lots of papers, research, the brain scans, and the four vials. I picked up one of the vials. It weighed nothing. I tilted it just to see the liquid shift around to prove to myself that there was something in there. I put it down, pushing the end slightly into the soil so it would stand up. What had Gene called it — BDNF. And then I remembered what those initials stood for — brain-derived neurotropic factor.

Really, this clear liquid was nothing more than a concentrated thing that was in every baby's brain — that had been in my brain when I was an infant. It wasn't dangerous. It was almost natural. But then, was being as smart as Gene natural? Were humans meant to be that smart?

"He's been gone a long time," I said to myself.

In all this excitement, all this danger, I was still feeling bored waiting. If I could have used my phone, I could have looked at some tweets or checked out Instagram or called Liv. I wondered what she was doing right now, what she thinking about all of this? What was everybody at school thinking about me? Were some of them being interviewed and saying things like "She was always so quiet" or "We never suspected" or worse "I always thought she could do something like that"?

Now at least it would be a little bit better. My parents and the police had my letter. Janice would have told her story and probably been interviewed, and that interview was probably playing in a continuous loop on the cable news networks. Hopefully everybody would now see me as a victim, a hostage, instead of an accomplice to murder. Gene had done that for me.

I just wished I at least had something to read to pass the time … Wait — I had a briefcase full of papers. I carefully removed a few documents and looked at the first page. There were charts and graphs, but mainly it was filled with words that I didn't recognize and had trouble pronouncing. I flipped to the second page. It was the same, as was the third. I put them back in their place in the briefcase and in doing so caught sight of the scanned images, and then I wondered — could I see on those scans what made Gene into Gene?

I held a scan up to allow the setting sun to shine through it and illuminate the image. Somehow, I thought there should be something different, something that would just stand out to the untrained eye. Then I realized there was a difference — it was the color. I'd seen my scans and knew there were white parts and gray parts. On this scan there was nothing but white. How could that be?

I took out a second image and did the same. Then a third. They were all identical — all of them were just white with no gray. There was still a stack of them. I pulled out another and then wondered, *What's the point of looking any further?*

I was just about to put the last scan away when I noticed it *was* different from the first three. When I compared them side by side, this one was smaller, and the shading was different. It had gray shading as well as the white areas. They were so different. I wondered if this was a "before" scan of how Gene's brain used to look before the serum was used. If only the images were dated, I could tell for sure. Wait, this one did have writing, right there on the bottom.

I looked at it, and my heart almost stopped. There was no date, but there was a name. My name. I was looking at one of my brain scans.

27

MY HAND WAS shaking as I tried to put everything back into the briefcase in an organized, methodical manner — like somehow establishing order would help me to think straight. It wasn't working. Instead, I felt numb. Not just my brain but my whole body. I couldn't even begin to understand why my brain scan images were in the briefcase, why they'd been in that lab in Gene's house. How did they get there, and why would his people want them? My head was spinning.

I looked at my watch. Gene had been gone for seventy-five minutes. I was getting worried. Getting *more* worried. I felt like I'd be worried for the rest of my life. Assuming there was a life in front of me. Okay, that made the worry start to inch up from anxiety to near panic.

I had a headache coming on, and it was getting stronger and stronger. Just the thing to make a bad situation worse. Then again, how could I describe any of this as just bad?

I caught sight of Gene and felt an instant sense of relief. He had come out the door and started his way across the runway and to the fence. He was moving with that same relaxed gait he always had. He reached the fence, dropped down, disappearing from view, and reappeared on my side. Now he moved faster, crouched over, and quickly reached my side and dropped to the dirt beside me.

"Sorry for taking so long."

"What now?"

"We wait until the flight that went out comes back and they close down for the night."

"How do you know that flight is coming back?" I asked.

"The door they came out of, the one I went into, is a flight school. That was a ninety-minute lesson — I read it in the log book — so they'll be back within a few minutes. I'm sorry I left you for so long and with responsibility for the briefcase. I'm so sorry for everything," Gene said.

"Everything?"

"Everything except you." He reached out and took my hand, and I felt a little better.

I wondered if I could ask him to apply pressure to my neck to make the headache go away. But there was one thing that I had to do first. I had to ask him about the scans — *my* scans. How could I do that without telling him I'd been snooping in his "ultra-secret" business? That made me more than a bad girlfriend: that made me a spy. But if I was a spy, what was he? He had my brain scans and hadn't told me. I needed to know.

"Becky, there are some things I have to tell you," he said. "Things you need to know."

I had the irrational thought that he'd just read my mind. That was impossible — or was it? Was that something Gene could do?

"I've told you more than I should have, but there are certain parts that concern you, and also parts that I'm going to have to tell you about before they happen."

"I understand that you couldn't tell me everything," I said.

"But I want to tell you everything. It's just that once I tell you things, they can't be untold. Some things will only put you more at risk."

"Sort of like ignorance is bliss."

"More like knowledge is dangerous. Look, I told you that I came here as part of an experiment. Nobleton was chosen because it was in the middle of nowhere. They thought it was a good location for this to take place without anybody finding out or finding me."

"I guess they were wrong about that," I said.

"They were wrong about lots of things." He paused. "Especially about getting you involved."

"They didn't get me involved. We fell in love."

"And that's when you became involved. Because we fell in love and because of your headaches."

"My headaches?"

"It's hard to explain everything, but I should have stopped what they were planning. I should have just said they couldn't do it. It's just that I didn't understand what they were doing at first and then when I did know, I didn't believe I could say no."

"I don't know what you mean. What does any of this have to do with my headaches?"

He looked at me as if he was studying me. "You have a headache right now."

"It's not a bad one."

"When we get inside, I'll apply pressure."

"When we get inside where?" I asked. "I thought we were stealing a plane."

"We are, but first we have to go into the flying school. And look, here comes the plane now."

He motioned to the south, and I looked but couldn't see anything. "I don't see it."

"It's still far away. Keep your eyes focused on the control tower and you'll see it off to the right."

I couldn't see anything. Then, as I kept staring, I saw a small dot in the sky, hardly visible at all. It got bigger and bigger until it was obviously a plane.

"It's the plane that originated from here, that went out for the flight lesson."

"How can you tell that? It's too far away."

"My sight is particularly acute."

"Nobody's sight is that good. I have twenty-twenty vision, perfect vision, and I can't tell if that's the same plane."

"You have normal vision," Gene said. "That means that you can see things at twenty feet that normal people can see at twenty feet."

"And your vision is better than that?" I asked.

"Twenty-two. I can see things at twenty feet that most people can see from two feet away. I can see the plane in the distance and tell that it's the plane that took off from here."

"Your eyes are different?"

"Not my eyes, but the processing of information. You don't see with your eyes or hear with your ears. You see and hear with your brain."

"And you can do that because of the serum?"

"The serum is only part of it. My brain is different from other people's. Do you know what myelin is?"

I shook my head.

"They call it miracle myelin because when it sheaths a neuron it processes information much faster."

"How much faster?" I asked.

"Up to twenty times. On a brain scan, myelin looks white as opposed to other areas that look gray."

Like his scans.

"And your brain has more white matter," I said. That wasn't a question. I knew because I'd seen it with my own eyes.

"Almost ninety-seven percent. Normal humans have slightly less than sixty percent."

"If you have more myelin, does that mean you're twenty times smarter than everybody else?" I asked.

"It's not that simple an equation. It's also how my brain reacts when given the serum."

"So, you could be *more* than twenty times smarter than me?"

"Let me try to explain." He paused and looked like he was thinking hard about what to say next.

"We moved here to have me involved with certain life experiences."

"What sort of experiences?" I asked.

"Just being around people, doing things that normal teenagers do, things I hadn't experienced because I was raised in isolation."

"So, they wanted to see how you'd interact with people."

"More than that. They wanted to know how those experiences would produce hormonal and enzyme reactions and see how they would impact the structural and functional changes to my brain."

"Are you saying being around people can change your brain?"

"Yes, it can and it does. And basically, the experiment was going very well in the beginning, but it changed." He paused. "There was an unexpected variable that changed the original experiment into something completely different."

"What happened?"

"I promise I'll explain it all, but first, I need to focus on the plane for a few minutes as it lands."

Did he really need to observe it, or was that just an excuse because he didn't know what to say or how to say it? Either way, I had no choice but to watch and wait.

The plane came in, lower and lower, and I saw and heard the wheels hit the pavement. The plane then jumped into the air again before settling back down on the runway.

"I think the instructor turned over the controls for his student to land," Gene explained.

The plane reached the end of the runway and taxied along to the spot where it had been sitting before. Now, at this distance, I could tell it was the same plane and the same two people who got out. As they walked away, we could hear animated, happy conversation. They went into the building, through the door Gene had used.

"Let me continue," Gene said. "The variable we didn't expect was you."

"Me?"

"And me. Me falling in love with you changed everything. It produced more dynamic changes in my brain."

"Are you saying I ruined the experiment?"

"Not ruined it. Changed it. Do you know how they say that people in love do stupid things?" he asked.

"I've seen it with my own eyes."

"It's real, and it's called romantic intoxication."

"It sounds like somebody is drunk or on drugs," I joked.

"It is drugs. We're nothing but drugs — enzymes and hormones. When somebody falls in love, their brain changes. It releases different chemicals, there are different reactions, and the brain starts to rewire."

"And they wanted to study that happening to you?" I asked.

"They had no choice. It was what was happening to my brain. And because they thought you were in love with me too, they wanted to study you as well."

"They were studying me?"

"They weren't examining just my brain functioning and structure but yours as well."

"What are you saying?" As soon as I said those words, I realized that was why they'd had my scans.

"When they found out you were having brain scans done, the project staff saw a chance to make you a control subject. They could see how somebody who wasn't part of the program, who hadn't been altered, would have their brain change when they fell in love," Gene explained. "They were looking at your brain scans as well. The ones before you met me and the ones that took place after."

"I don't know what to say, what to think," I stammered.

"How could you? This is all beyond anything that's comprehensible. It had to be kept from me to keep the experiment pure. It wasn't until later, when I stumbled across one of your scans in the lab, that I suspected what they were doing. I demanded to know what was happening. I told them they had to stop or else I'd quit the program. That was what was happening when I missed those last days at school."

"I had no idea. It's just so hard to understand. Us falling in love was just an experiment."

"No, it was never just an experiment!" he exclaimed. "They tried to make it into an experiment. It wasn't. It isn't. It's the most amazing, unbelievable, inexplicable thing that's ever happened to me. *You're* the most amazing, unbelievable, inexplicable thing that's ever happened to me."

I felt my whole body start to tingle.

"But that's how you became part of the experiment," he said.

"And that's why you have my MRI scans in the briefcase."

He looked shocked. "I didn't know you knew that."

"I saw them when you were in the building."

"I wish I could have told you before you found them. I felt terrible about not telling you; it felt like I was lying to you."

"You were lying to me."

"I wanted to tell you, but I was afraid," he said.

"Afraid of what?"

"Afraid that you'd think that I'd been the one who tricked you and made you a part of the experiment without your permission or knowledge."

"I just don't understand. How could they do that to me? How could it be legal?"

"You have to understand, there's no legal or illegal. What I'm part of, what you became part of, it's all above the law."

"It feels like you were ordered to fall in love with me."

"I wasn't — they couldn't! They just told me they wanted to observe me interacting with other people my age. That was how it all started. And that was all it was supposed to be. You have to believe me."

I didn't know what to say.

"Me falling in love with you just happened. Like magic. I fell in love with you, and it was real and genuine. The most real thing that has ever happened to me." He paused. "I was afraid, I'm still afraid, that once you found out what was behind all of this, you wouldn't love me anymore."

He looked so sad, so desperate, so scared. I felt like my heart was sinking. I reached out and took his hand.

"Do you think I can fall in and out of love that easily?" I asked.

He shrugged. "The only thing I know less about than humor is love."

"I guess I'm lucky you fell in love with me and not somebody else," I said.

"That would have been impossible. It was you from the beginning. There's just something about you. It had to be you."

"And I'm supposed to believe that?"

"You know it's true. Love is beyond science or reason. It just is. It knocked me off my feet. *You* knocked me off my feet."

I laughed. "It sounds like suddenly you do believe in fate or magic."

"Science brought me here. Falling in love with you was fate. Love is magic."

"How did they get my scans?"

"Becky, they can do anything. There's a level of things going on that's beyond anything people understand. They can access all records, hack all computers, listen to all phone calls. There's nothing they don't know and no place they can't reach."

"How about this cornfield?"

"We're safe for now, but not much longer. There are satellites being repositioned over us. There are people on the ground and drones in the sky searching for us. Some want to hurt us, and some want to save us."

I couldn't help but look up. All I could see were the puffy, white clouds.

"And we can't tell who's on what side. That's why we have to get away from here quickly. The longer we stay, the more the walls close in on all sides. But there's something else you have to know: I will not let anybody harm you. I would sacrifice my life for you. I love you with all my heart."

There was so much that seemed beyond belief, but what Gene just said … well, I had no doubts about that.

28

WE WAITED UNTIL the two men left the building. At six o'clock, the lights in the tower went off, and then we waited another fifteen minutes just to make sure. Gene circled around the airport outside the fence on foot and watched as three cars left and somebody locked the gate behind them. I stayed in the corn and looked upward for unseen satellites and planes and drones.

We moved across the deserted tarmac to the building. Gene turned the doorknob and rattled the door.

"Is it locked?"

"Yes, but when I was inside, I took the spare key."

He pulled it out of his pocket, inserted it in the lock, and opened the door. Inside, it was dark, and he ushered me in, closing the door behind us. I could barely see the nose at the end of my face. I felt his hand take mine.

"We'll move slowly. Follow behind. My eyes don't need as much light as yours."

"Are you a cat?"

"Not that sensitive."

But better than other human beings. Like a different species. That was such a *stupid* thing to think. He just had better vision.

We edged forward, me seeing nothing, guided by his hand in

mine. Then a big overhead light came on. We were in a room with chairs, a couple of couches, a big television mounted on the wall, and, most importantly, four solid walls; there were no outside windows.

"There's a fridge under that counter with some food and lots of bottled water. Drink and eat and then fill our bottles," Gene said.

"And what are you going to do?"

"I'm going to learn to fly."

"Funny. Really, what are you going to do?"

"I'm going to learn to fly a small single-engine airplane."

"Because you already know how to fly a large two-engine plane?"

"Becky, I've only ever *been* in a plane once in my life. I'm going to learn how to fly. That's why we're in the flight school."

"Let me get this straight. We're going to steal a plane and you're going to fly it even though you have no idea how to fly a plane. Is that correct?"

"Partially correct. I know everything about the dynamics involved in flight. What I don't is how to fly a plane. I'm going to learn. We'll leave within two hours."

"You're saying you're going to learn how to fly a plane in two hours."

"It'll be closer to ninety minutes. The first thirty minutes are preparation to begin the learning process."

"This is crazy. Gene, nobody can take a plane up after ninety minutes. Well, and hope to live."

"Becky, do you remember the day I told you I could play the saxophone?"

"Of course, in the music room."

"I'd never even held one before that day."

"That can't be true. You're an amazing saxophone player."

"I learned how to play in the two days after that. Do you remember the day in the gym that I went to talk to you and I threw the ball at the net and it dropped?"

"Of course."

"That was the first time I'd ever held a basketball. You always joke that I'm a fast learner, but that's not true. I'm an almost *instant* learner. Between the serum and the extra white matter of my brain, I can learn things faster than any other human being can. Faster than any human being ever could in history."

"That's not possible."

"You've heard me play the saxophone, and you've seen me on the court."

"But this isn't playing an instrument or shooting some hoops, this is about flying a plane."

"Which is fundamentally much easier to do than either of those."

"But you can't even drive a stick shift!" I exclaimed.

"I can't drive any car, but that's because I haven't attempted to learn that skill. I did attempt to learn how to play the saxophone and basketball."

"But even then, it took you days to learn those skills, and you're talking about ninety minutes to learn to fly a plane," I said.

"I wasn't authorized to learn to play basketball or saxophone. That's why they took me so long."

"I don't understand."

"I did those *without* the use of the serum. Those weren't things that were authorized by the program scientists — my parents or the other people running the program."

"Those were because of your brain being different?"

"Exactly. Now I'm going to use the serum so I can learn to fly. It will be so much quicker. You have to have faith. It keeps coming back to the same question: Do you trust me?"

"I wouldn't be here if I didn't."

"And I'm going to have to trust you. You're going to see something that nobody outside our research team has ever witnessed. You're going to be present when I use the serum."

Gene put down the briefcase on a coffee table. He clicked it open and removed a vial. He brought it up toward his face and stared at it.

"The vial has dirt on it."

"When you left me in the field, I took them out," I said. "I wanted to have them right at hand in case I needed to destroy them if somebody surprised me."

"That makes sense."

"I guess I was also curious."

He reached back into the briefcase and pulled out a syringe with a hypodermic needle.

I had no doubt, but I still had to ask. "You're going to inject it?"

"That's how it gets into my system." He paused. "But there are some side effects that you need to know about. I don't want you to be afraid of what you're going to see, because I've been told it can be disturbing."

Now he had me scared. "Wait … but if you've been injected,

then you've seen your reactions."

"One of the first reactions is that I'm going to lose consciousness. I'm going to present as if I'm having a seizure. It's very possible that I'm going to froth at the mouth."

"Maybe you shouldn't do it."

"Without the serum, it would take me days to learn to fly a plane. We don't have days. Besides, it's far from the first time I've been injected with the serum."

"How many times have there been?"

"This will be number two hundred and eighty-nine. It's all been completely documented. Each time. This one will ultimately also be entered into the formal data when we reach the facility."

"But you're going to be okay?"

"Within thirty minutes it'll be like it never happened."

He took the vial and plunged the needle in through the top and pulled the plunger up. The syringe filled with the clear liquid. He'd taken about half of the vial. He looked closely at the syringe and tapped it with his finger.

"Are you ready for me to do this?" he asked.

"I'm ready." What else could I say?

"Normally the injection would be given right here," he said, putting a finger to the back of his neck, just in the hairline. "But I can't do that myself, and I wouldn't want you to have to do it."

Thank goodness.

He sat down on the couch and proceeded to remove his left shoe and sock. He bent over and put the syringe in the gap between his big toe and the next toe. He inserted the needle, and I felt my whole body shudder. He pushed down on the plunger and then removed the needle.

"There, simple as that." He put the half-filled vial back into the briefcase. "I have to lie down now."

He stretched out on the couch. He was so long that his feet hung slightly over the end.

"This might be a good time for you to get something to eat and drink."

I was hungry and thirsty. I went over to the little fridge and opened the door. There were a dozen bottles of water. I took out two.

"Do you want one?"

"It's better that my stomach is empty in case I vomit."

"That could happen?" I asked.

"It can. This is going to look bad, but it will pass quickly."

I almost said, "And if it doesn't?" but instead I just smiled and nodded my head reassuringly. Who was I trying to reassure, him or me?

"How long before it takes effect?" I asked.

"I'm starting to feel it right now. I'm just going to close my eyes and wait."

"Do you want me to turn off the lights?"

"Soon you'll be able to shine a spotlight in my face and I won't react."

He lay there, his arms under his head, eyes closed, stretched out. He looked like he was lying down for a nap. And then his body started to shake — ever so slightly at first, and then much stronger.

"Gene, are you all right?"

There was no answer. I called out again, this time louder. Still no response.

The shaking got worse, and then suddenly his eyes opened, but there were no pupils or irises. His eyes had rolled back in his head. His mouth was open and foaming. It was happening just the way he'd warned me. I was watching something happen to Gene that he'd never seen himself.

The shaking intensified. Sweat beaded his forehead. I reached down and wiped his brow with my hand. He was hot to the touch. It was like I was watching a storm taking place in his body. I reached out again, took his hand in mine, and held it tightly. He wasn't going to fight the storm alone.

29

GENE'S SWEATING STOPPED and the fever broke, but I kept running a cloth under cold water and using it to wipe his brow. I thought the cold would still feel good. I moved the syringe off to the side.

I was feeling so alone. So helpless. I wanted my parents. I wanted to call them, but I knew I couldn't. If those men weren't monitoring their phones, then the FBI or some spy agency probably was. Besides, I knew I couldn't even turn my phone on or they'd be able to track us.

I looked over. There on the desk was a black phone. A landline. Nobody would be tracking this line. They'd be tracking my phone, and they might be tracking my parents' phone, but it wasn't my parents I had in mind. I had to think of the number. My phone was programmed with everybody's numbers so I never had to memorize anything.

I picked up the phone, and it hummed. We didn't have a home phone, and it took a split second to realize that was the sound that it was working. I punched in the numbers and hoped they were right. It rang and rang and rang and —

"No, we don't want to buy anything." It was Liv.

"It's me. It's Becky."

"My goodness … I didn't recognize the number — are you okay?"

"I'm okay. We're both okay."

"What happened?"

"I can't explain it. You know we didn't hurt anybody."

"I know, but what did happen?"

"I can't explain it, and if I did you wouldn't believe it."

I heard a voice in the background. "Who's on the phone?" It was Liv's dad.

"It's, um, Emma!" she yelled back. "Where are you?" she said to me.

"It might as well be another planet, but I can't tell you that either."

"Is there anything I can do?"

"Yes, could you tell my parents I'm safe?"

"I'll call them as soon as I get off the phone with you."

"No, you can't call them. You have to go and tell them. I'm sure their phones are bugged. And could you wait a couple of hours so we're even farther away?"

"Okay, I'll do that. Please be safe."

"We're trying. Gene's taking care of me."

"And he didn't kidnap you?"

"Of course not. Liv, I have to go. I love you."

"I love you too, Becky."

"Goodbye." I hung up. There was nothing else to say.

I looked at my watch for what seemed like the hundredth time. It had now been around twenty-eight minutes since he had injected. I wasn't exactly sure because I hadn't thought to even look at the time for three or four minutes after it had happened. Gene had said that it would all be over in thirty minutes. I wasn't expecting it to be like an alarm sounding when the half-hour mark was reached, but it still gave me something to hope for.

It had been terrible to watch. Especially to watch happening to somebody whom you loved. Love. That's how I felt. I was in love with him. This boy — this man — who I didn't even know existed a short while ago was somebody I was in love with. There was so much about him that was a mystery. He was like an onion. Layer after layer kept peeling off, but how many more layers were still to come? Was he holding back, only revealing things as he thought I could handle them? How much more would I need to know? How many more layers could I even handle?

"Hello, Becky." Gene was looking at me. Eyes open, smiling.

"How are you feeling?" I asked.

"A little weak, but that passes quickly. Soon I'm going to have a power surge and an incredible feeling that overwhelms my senses."

"What's it like?"

"I've thought about that a lot over the years. It's pretty amazing. Imagine that your entire life you've only been able to see in black and white. And then suddenly you can see in color."

"That *would* be pretty amazing."

"Only it's not just color but vibrant, vivid, brilliant colors. Colors that aren't even in the range that normal human beings can see. And you can't just see the colors, you can *smell* them, and you can't just smell them, but you can taste them in your mouth and hear them in your ears. And the colors aren't just outside of you, they're inside of you as well."

"I can't even imagine that."

"There's only one thing that even compares," Gene said.

"What's that?"

"Falling in love."

I laughed. "Nice to know I'm in second place."

He sat up. "First place. I wouldn't trade you for all of this. You've changed my world, not to mention my brain functioning and structure."

"Before, when we talked, before all of this, were you thinking of offering me the serum so I could study for my SATs?"

He looked embarrassed but nodded his head ever so slightly.

"Of course, I would have told you all about it, explained the consequences and the side effects. It would have been your choice."

"But would your parents have let you do that?" I asked.

"I would have done it without them knowing."

"But if they'd found out, what would have happened?"

"I can't even think about that now. I have to learn to fly a plane."

Gene got up and walked over to a bookshelf and removed a big, black binder. He sat down at a table, opened up the binder, and swept his hand down the first page, then turned to the next. Page after page, in the time it took for his hand to sweep from top to bottom, he was processing the information.

There was no point in me watching anymore. I needed to get water and food. The two bottles were still on the counter. I brought one over to Gene, who didn't seem to notice it or me. I went back and drank from the second bottle. I tipped it back and drank and drank and drank until it was drained. I hadn't realized just how thirsty I was.

I took a second bottle and poked around in the fridge. There were some cold cuts in a plastic bag, a half-eaten sandwich, some poppy seed bagels, and a donut box. I opened up the box, and there were still four donuts. This was where I was going to start.

I pulled out a chocolate one. I could tell from the touch it wasn't fresh, but it was still a donut. I ate the whole thing and grabbed a second that had sprinkles. Three bites and it was gone. I took another big drink of water. I reached for a third donut but pulled back, realizing I should leave the last two for Gene. I put the box on the counter and grabbed the plastic bag of bagels. I hoped they'd be fresher, but really, it didn't matter.

I looked at the television mounted on the wall and wondered if I could turn it on. I grabbed the remote control from the coffee table and aimed at the set. It came to life — it was a sports high- light show, bloopers of the day. The volume was almost off. I went to turn it up but stopped. Gene always talked about not being distracted when he was inputting information, and I certainly didn't want to have this information inputted incorrectly. This was about a lot more than getting a good mark on a test.

I moved to within two feet of the set, and I could hear the unseen announcer describing the action as a basketball player got hit in the side of the head by a pass he didn't know was coming. It was sort of funny but not what I wanted.

I scrolled through the channels until I found the one the dis- play identified as CNN, which was on a break and showing a commercial for some drug. Every second commercial on CNN seemed to be about a drug. This one was like all the others, showing a lovely scene with old-looking people doing all sorts of amazing activities that were probably too dangerous for somebody even my age to do. Although, none of them was going to go up in an airplane with somebody who was learning to fly in ninety minutes.

The man on his surfboard faded away and was replaced by the warning. Apparently, this drug could cause a whole bunch of things, including headaches, bleeding, heart attacks, and death. Why did every drug seem to have so many side effects? Wait, what side effects did the serum have? I'd seen what it caused in the short term — the seizures — but what about the long term? And then CNN came back on.

There, staring at me, were our pictures. Mine was my school picture from last year. God, I wished I'd done something better with my hair. That was such a ridiculous thought. Gene's picture was cropped from a group photo with the basketball team. The faces of teammates around him had been blurred out.

The talking heads — a man and a woman at the desk — began speaking.

"As reported in our last segment with a local sergeant from the state police, the net is closing around the vicinity of Nobleton, Indiana," the female announcer said.

"The authorities are warning people to keep doors and windows closed and locked after one home was invaded and the occupant, Mrs. Janice Coventry, tied up as the pair stole the family pickup and fled," the man added.

"If you do see them, do not approach, but contact the police," the female anchor said.

"Originally it was believed that police were seeking two suspects. As reported earlier, it is now believed that the female, Becky James, is in fact a hostage," the male reporter added.

"Gene, you should hear this!" I said as I turned around.

He didn't respond. He was transfixed by what he was doing. I turned back to the television.

"We are going to take you, live and on location, to Nobleton," the male anchor said.

The screen split in two to continue to show the two anchors but also a reporter standing beside a woman — it was Mrs. Edleman, the administrator at the nursing home! They were in the dining hall.

The reporter introduced Mrs. Edleman and herself and gave their location.

"How long have you known Becky?"

"*Rebecca* has been volunteering here once or twice a week for over a year."

"And how would you describe her?"

"Hard-working. Friendly. Very positive. She's liked by the staff and all the residents, even those who might be described as a bit difficult."

I let out a little sigh of relief.

Along the bottom of the screen, the ticker described us as "Romeo and Juliet on the run." That would have been romantic if I hadn't known how that story ended.

"What did you think when you heard the news that Becky was a suspect in a double murder?" the interviewer asked.

"Of course, I was shocked, but never for a second did I believe Rebecca would be capable of doing those things."

I really did have to thank her — if I ever saw her again.

"Then you must have been relieved when it became known that she was simply a hostage."

Mrs. Edleman shook her head and scowled. "If you think a young girl being taken hostage is a source of relief, you certainly have no understanding of this situation."

The reporter's mouth dropped open, and her eyes widened. She looked like a deer caught in the headlights of an oncoming car. The reporter finally mumbled something, and the station cut back to the anchor desk.

"Stephen Davidson is also in Nobleton at another location. He's live at Westfield High School, which the two teens attend, and he's speaking to the basketball coach," the female anchor said.

Another change, and there was Coach towering over a reporter. The reporter was in a suit, dressed like he was going to a wedding. Coach was, as always, in his sweats.

"Coach Wilkins, this must be a shock to all the students of your school but would be particularly hard felt by the members of your basketball team."

"Big shock to us all."

"Becky was your team manager, and Gene is, I understand, one of your star players."

"Becky *is* our manager, and we don't have *star* players we just have *team* players."

Even on CNN, Coach remained Coach, saying the things he always said to his players. I wouldn't have been surprised if he'd made the reporter run sprints if he didn't like his questions.

"But he certainly was your leading scorer," the reporter said.

"What you have to know is that Gene is more than a good player, he's a good kid and —"

"But in truth, Coach, you've only known him a few weeks."

Coach did not look pleased at being cut off. "How long do you figure it takes to decide if somebody is a good person?" he asked. "I can get a pretty good idea about whether I like somebody in the time it takes to start an interview."

Oh, big shot! Both he and Mrs. Edleman were born and raised in Indiana, and we Indianans pride ourselves on being pretty direct about things. We don't like fancy or fake.

"It's reported that prior to attending Westfield, Gene had never previously attended school," the reporter said, not missing a beat.

"You could never tell by the way he fit in with his teammates."

"I've been told by others that Gene was described as unusual, different, and even socially awkward."

"And that would make him an average teenager," Coach replied.

"There are reports that he was obsessed with Becky and that perhaps that was the cause of the murder and abduction," he said.

"Don't you want to put the words *alleged* or *suspected* in front of those accusations?"

Way to go, Coach.

"Weren't you a teenager once?" Coach asked.

The reporter now looked confused. "Yes, of course."

"They were girlfriend and boyfriend. They liked to talk and spend time with each other. If you call that obsession, well, then yeah, they were obsessed with each other. Sure, if that's the *story* you need to *sell*."

Obviously, CNN didn't understand Indiana. My father had said more than once that he thought that cable news — whether it was CNN or Fox — could "make a peanut butter and jelly sandwich into a national emergency."

"Thank you for your time, Coach Wilkins. This is Stephen Davidson, reporting from Nobleton."

The screen went back to the anchor desk again and then quickly to commercial break.

It was a youngish-looking older couple sitting side by side in matching bathtubs on a lawn, and they were holding hands. I'd heard enough. I clicked off the television.

I turned around. Gene was in the far corner, and it looked like he was playing a video game. Then I realized he was flying a virtual airplane. The game was some sort of flight simulator.

Quietly, I crept up beside him. The screen showed the instrumentation of a small plane, and through the windshield was the ground below. Gene held a controller, and it looked like he was getting ready to land as a runway came into view. Lower and lower the plane came until it touched down, bounced slightly into the air, slowed down, and came to a stop.

"That looked good," I said.

"The flight manual said that any landing that you walk away from is a good landing, although I think they were joking."

"Definitely a joke. I'm hoping you'll be able to fly better than you can joke."

"I think I've passed that threshold. We should go."

I thought about telling him I'd called Liv but decided not to talk about anything that would distract him from flying. At least, that was what I told myself; my gut was telling me that Gene would be upset if he knew about the phone call.

"Let me get some more bottles of water and the bag of bagels, and there are a couple of donuts for you."

"How much do you think those things are worth?" he asked.

"Um … six bottles of water, bagels, stale donuts … maybe ten dollars?"

"Then I'll leave a thousand and ten dollars."

"What?"

"Money for those items, the fuel we're going to burn, and unauthorized plane rental. Being called a murderer and kidnapper is one thing, but I don't want to be called a thief." He started to smirk. "How's that for a joke?"

"You're definitely getting funnier."

"Coach didn't seem to like that reporter very much," Gene said.

"I didn't know you heard."

"I was listening. When you see him again, could you thank him for me?"

"The best way you can thank him is to get back in uniform and win him some games."

Gene smiled, but it was a sad smile. I understood what he was saying even when he wasn't talking. He wasn't going to be able to go back no matter what happened.

"I think we'd better get going," he said.

30

GENE CIRCLED THE aircraft. He was examining it, as the other two men had done before they took off earlier in the day, except Gene was using one of the two flashlights we'd borrowed — or, I guess, bought — from the flight school. I was reassured that I'd already seen this plane take off and land and knew it was flight-worthy. That was why he'd selected this plane. All I had to worry about was having a pilot who'd just learned to fly and had never flown anything before except a flight simulator. But this wasn't just some random guy, this was Gene. He was different from anybody else in the world. He'd injected himself with the serum and — then I had a terrible thought.

"Gene, the syringe you used to inject the serum, where is it?"

He shook his head. "It's still inside. I'll have to go get it. There will be traces of the serum still in it, so we can't let it be found."

"I'll go. You keep getting us ready to fly."

"That's a better idea. I want to top up the gas tank before we fly."

I hurried across the tarmac, keeping my flashlight off. The darkness gave me comfort, knowing I couldn't be seen by prying eyes. Of course, darkness wouldn't hide me from infrared imaging from a satellite that could see my heat signature.

I entered the building and clicked on the flashlight, then went down the corridor and into the big room. I found the syringe sitting on the coffee table. I hurried over and carefully picked it up. I moved the syringe around in the beam of light, trying to look inside. There was a drop or two left. Was that enough to analyze and reproduce the serum? And then I had an even stranger thought: What would happen if I injected those drops into me? I couldn't even go there in my mind right now. I carefully slipped the syringe into the side pocket of my backpack and hurried out, closing the door behind me.

Outside, I was greeted by the roar of an engine. The lights were on, and the blades of the propeller were whirling around. I made my way around the plane and opened the door, climbing up and in beside Gene. I turned off the flashlight and put my pack onto the floor.

Gene motioned for me to put on a headset. I slipped it on, and the roar of the engine was muffled.

"Is that better?" Gene said.

There were obviously communications built in. I fiddled with a little microphone at the end of a wire and pulled it down toward my mouth. "Better. You can hear me, right?"

"Roger that."

He leaned over and started to buckle me in. It wasn't just a lap belt — there was also a harness that went over both shoulders and another belt that came up from below. They clicked into a circular lock in the middle.

The engines roared louder, and we started bumping forward. We were going to taxi for takeoff. I was going to be taken up by a guy who had never flown a plane before. I had to fight the urge to tell him to stop, to let me out. I didn't. I couldn't. We picked up speed.

"Have you flown much?" Gene asked.

"A few times, but nothing this small. Just big jets."

"Sorry, there isn't something larger for me to borrow."

"Could you fly something bigger?"

"I can fly anything where I can read the manual. At least, that's the theory."

He took one hand off the control and took one of my hands. "Don't worry."

"I'm always worried on planes. I don't like flying."

"Just think: You've never been on a plane where the pilot just completely memorized the manual. I know this plane as well as the person who designed it."

"I believe — Look!" I exclaimed. "There are lights coming down the road."

They were close but still in the distance.

"Who do you think it could be?"

"Most likely just somebody passing by, but we might have tripped an alarm. It doesn't matter now. They can't stop us."

We came to the end of the runway. He spun the plane around so that we were facing the entire length ahead of us. I turned around so I could see the oncoming vehicle. It wasn't just one car.

"There are two — no, three vehicles! And they're getting closer, fast."

The engine roared, and we started to pick up speed. The first car — it was a big SUV — came barreling through the gate.

I couldn't help but scream. "They're coming, they're coming!"

We continued to pick up speed, but the vehicles were already on the runway, and they were gaining on us. They spread out so they were three vehicles wide, three sets of bright lights coming down the runway behind us, getting closer.

"Hurry, hurry, hurry!" I yelled.

They closed in until they were no more than a few car lengths behind us. Two of the vehicles went wide until there was one on either side of us. The back window of the car on my side rolled down. A man leaned out, pointing a gun. There was a flash and a bang that I could hear over the roar of the engine.

"He's firing, he's firing, he's firing at us!"

There were three more bursts.

"Get down," Gene yelled.

I ducked down at the same instant the plane rose into the air. We passed over the fence at the end of the runway, and I looked back and saw the three vehicles skid and slide to a stop. We'd gotten away.

31

"WHO WERE THOSE people?!" I screamed as the plane continued to rise higher and higher.

"I know they weren't the police, because the police don't just fire at people. I think they were from the same organization that invaded my house. But I'm not sure how they could have found us. When I was unconscious you didn't use your phone to call anybody, did you?"

"No, I didn't use my phone. I used the flight school phone so they couldn't track the tower or things like that."

"But they certainly have your parents' phones tapped."

"I didn't call my parents. I called Liv."

"You shouldn't have called anybody."

"I'm sorry ... I'm so sorry."

There were no words. The cabin was filled with the roar of the engine.

"I understand," he said. "You were scared. I was unconscious, and you felt alone."

"And I wanted her to tell my parents I was okay. I shouldn't have called. I won't do that again."

He put a hand on my knee. "You didn't know. We got away. But still, I'm going dark."

The outside lights stopped flashing, and the dashboard lights went out.

"Can you please push the red button in the middle of that thing that looks like a radio?" Gene asked. It was the only light left on the dashboard.

"Do you really want music?"

"It's not a radio. It's a transponder. It sends out an electronic ping that shows our location. It's a safety feature on planes so they can be tracked. We don't want to be tracked."

I pushed the button, and the transponder went as dark as the rest of the controls.

The plane banked to one side, and I put one hand on the door and the other on the dashboard to steady myself.

"I just can't believe they were shooting at us," I said.

"They weren't shooting at *us*. They were shooting at the *plane*, trying to disable it."

"How can you be so sure of that?"

"From that distance, if they'd wanted us dead, we'd be dead. They wanted to capture me alive."

"But they said they could kill you and cut open your head to get the serum."

"They were trying to scare me into cooperating."

"The cooperating thing didn't work, but I was pretty scared," I said.

"Hang on. I'm about to do a hard bank. We've been traveling in the wrong direction while they could see us, and now I'll take us in the right direction."

"To the east, toward New York?"

"Yes. I'm going to bank sharp to the starboard side. Hang on."

The wing on my side rose up, and we started to turn. I couldn't see the ground, only the sky above.

"How are you able to tell where to fly in the dark?"

"I'm navigating from star positions."

"You can do that?"

"Along with reading flight manuals and the specific controls of this plane, I also read about celestial navigation. It's not difficult once you memorize the star map, factor in the time, and apply basic trigonometry. You can easily plot from the stars."

"Yeah, that sounds *really* simple. How fast are we traveling?"

"Slightly under one hundred and twenty miles per hour."

"So, we could get to New York State within five or six hours."

"We could if we were flying in a straight line. I'm flying a course that avoids major airports that would have a radar array. I don't want to show up as an unidentified blip on somebody's screen. They might think I'm a UFO or something. By the way, did you tell Liv I didn't kidnap you and take you back to my home planet?"

"You know about her saying things like that?"

"I overheard her. It's not just my eyes that work better," he said.

"Is that why you always talked about the school being so loud?"

"That was part of it."

"And you can do all of this because of the serum?"

"The serum is part of it. The different brain structure is a bigger part."

"That's the extra white matter in your brain, that myelin stuff, right?" I asked.

"The interaction between the two, combined with the multi-sensory learning techniques, produces the results."

"What would happen if I were injected with the serum?"

"It would dramatically, exponentially increase your ability to input, retain, and retrieve information."

"But it wouldn't work the same way for me, would it? I wouldn't be able to fly a plane after ninety minutes."

"No. You have to think of the serum as special fuel and the white matter as the engine."

"And my engine isn't as powerful as yours. Nobody's is as powerful as yours, is it?" I asked.

He didn't answer.

"Is your brain ten times bigger than my tiny brain?"

"My brain isn't physically any larger, and your brain is not tiny."

"But your brain is more powerful."

"I process, retain, retrieve, and utilize information faster than anybody else can."

"Anybody in the world."

He nodded. "Any human that's ever lived."

I let those words sink in. Gene was smarter than Einstein or da Vinci … and so much smarter than me. Like another species. And then I had a question.

"How much smarter am I than a chimpanzee?"

"Much smarter. The flexibility of the brain, the ability to utilize language, and the general structure, including a larger proportion of myelin in human brains."

"What percentage of a chimp's brain is myelin?"

"Approximately forty percent," he answered.

"So, if your brain is close to one hundred percent, and my brain is around sixty, then I'm closer to a chimp than I am to you."

"No. For starters, the human brain is three times as large as a chimpanzee's, so you have to divide that forty percent by three," he explained.

"Okay, so the chimp comes in around thirteen percent, which means that I'm still not that much closer to you than I am to a chimp."

"It's much more complicated than that," Gene protested. "And your ability to learn would be greatly enhanced by the serum."

"But even if I took the serum, I still wouldn't be as smart as you because you have so much more myelin. Even if I get the same fuel, my engine will always be smaller, right?"

"Additional myelin can only be produced by altering genetics to produce more NGF — nerve growth factor — in utero."

"So, either you're born with it or you're not," I said.

He nodded his head. "The increase in my myelin was triggered by CRISPR."

"A what?"

"It's a programmable method for modifying DNA. People call it gene splicing. They can use it to change eye or hair color, or to eliminate genes that cause illness or diseases like multiple sclerosis or Parkinson's disease or —"

"Or to make somebody so smart that he's not like anybody else in the world."

He nodded. "Yes, gene splicing was used to produce that myelin growth in me."

"And they could do this with all babies?" I asked.

"Technically, but it's expensive and complicated, and they don't know all of the possible consequences."

"What sort of consequences?"

"Any time you try something new, there are always things you can't anticipate, unintended consequences that could negatively impact or even kill the recipient."

"But with you, they just made you *better* than anybody else."

"Not better. Different. I'm just different."

"Are there others like you, or are you the only one?"

"We're *all* the only one. Each of us is unique."

"You know what I mean," I said.

"I'm one of a kind."

"Is that what that man meant when he said you were a different species?" I asked.

"That's what he wants to believe, but I'm still just human. People are afraid of what's different, and my brain is different. Besides, unless I can reproduce the changes in my brain structure in the brains of my offspring, it isn't as significant."

"What do you mean, reproduce?"

"You know I've been altered genetically. However, the changes made in me would be so much more important if those changes, my genetic alterations, such as the additional myelin, would be passed down to my offspring."

"In your children," I said.

"Exactly, but we won't know that for more than a decade. I'm not scheduled to attempt to procreate until I'm in my early thirties."

"You have a schedule to have children?"

"I have a schedule for everything. Now, I have to make some course corrections, so can you excuse me while I try to figure out the star positions? I need full concentration."

"Sure, no problem."

"Becky, this is going to be a long flight. You should probably try to get some sleep."

"I can try."

I slumped down in my seat and closed my eyes. Again, more information to process. Gene was made different. Did that make him a different species? How much smarter was he than me or everybody else in the world? Was he forty times as smart as me, or was it much more? Was I forty times as smart as a dog? Probably not a poodle.

I felt the vibration of the engine rumbling through my body. It was soothing, relaxing. Despite everything, maybe I could sleep.

32

I OPENED MY eyes, and it took a few seconds for it all to come back to me. The only thing reassuring me was that Gene had placed a hand on my leg.

I'd slept, but it had been a troubled sleep full of dead bodies and running from people trying to catch me. It was a nightmare, but what made it much worse was that it was also real. Waking up didn't put it behind me.

"How long have I been asleep?"

"Just over six hours."

That meant that we'd traveled at least seven hundred miles since I'd dropped off.

"Where are we?"

"We just entered New York State airspace. We're between Buffalo and Rochester. Those lights to our left are Batavia."

I could see faint lights coming from houses or buildings.

"I've never heard of it."

"Batavia is a city in Genesee County. According to the latest census data, it has a population of sixteen thousand, two hundred and fifty-six people. Its motto is 'Right Place, Right Time.'"

"How do you know that?"

"I memorized all the population centers and geography along our flight plan. To our right is the New York State Thruway, and those lights are vehicles traveling along it."

"It's almost pretty."

"Not nearly as pretty as you."

"Sure, I must be really pretty after sleeping in a shed and now in a plane, both without a shower, unable to comb my hair, and with two-day-old makeup smeared and caked on."

"You're right. Pretty was the wrong word. Beautiful is the right one."

"I know you're lying, but thanks for the reassuring lie."

"No lie. Besides, you saw me at my worst after I took the serum."

"You told me what to expect, but it's hard to see that happen to somebody that you care for."

"Care for?" Gene asked. "I thought we'd moved beyond that."

"Fine. It's hard to see that happen to somebody you love."

"So much better. Besides, you'd be crazy to go through all of this with somebody you just cared for."

"I'm still pretty crazy to go through all of this with somebody I love."

"I wish you hadn't been there when it all happened," Gene said.

"If it wasn't for me and that field hockey stick, you never would have gotten away to begin with. I was meant to be there."

"I shouldn't have let you come along. I should have eliminated those two men so nobody would know that you were there," he said.

"I couldn't let you do that."

"I put you in a terrible position, and I keep putting you in more bad spots, like knowing about the serum, having seen me administer it. Nobody outside of the research team has ever witnessed that."

"How many injections did you tell me you've had?" I asked.

"Two hundred and eighty-nine."

"That's a lot of injections."

"What choice did I have?"

There was something wistful about the way he said that. Did he mean that they hadn't given him a choice?

"Are we flying all the way to the compound?" I asked.

"They have a helipad, but they don't have an airstrip for a fixed-wing craft. There's a field where we can land about five miles away. With any luck, we'll be in the compound within a few hours."

I let out a big sigh.

"We'll be safe, and I can explain to them that I didn't kill Dr. Lawrence and Dr. Wilson," he said.

"But they know you'd never do that, right?"

He didn't answer.

"They have to know that you would never do that."

There was a silence before he spoke. "Becky, I've never committed any act of violence. You have to believe that."

"I believe that." I felt a sense of relief.

"But there are so many things you don't know."

I waited for him to go on.

"I'm not the first to be re-engineered. I'm the fourth."

"There are four people like you?"

"Not like me. Different. All of them showed increased intelligence, but there were side effects. Two showed violent tendencies. One of them hurt people. The second, well, he killed somebody."

"That's awful."

"There's more. The third took his own life," Gene said.

"He killed himself? Are they sure it wasn't an accident?"

"I saw the tape, read the letter he left. There's no question. I think there's reason for them to believe that I'm capable of violence."

"You're not. I know that."

"We're all capable of violence. I just don't think I'm any more or less capable than anybody else."

The engine seemed to flutter and stall slightly, the roar of the engine fading before getting louder again.

I looked over at Gene.

"It's done that before," he said. "I'm going to take us higher."

"Wait, I thought we were going to stay low to be under radar."

"I flew low until we were well south of Buffalo, but I decided I had to chance going higher because the engine has been running rough. I wonder if those bullets that were fired at us might have caused some damage."

"You think the plane is damaged?" I demanded.

"I don't know, but that's why I wanted to gain elevation."

"If something is wrong, shouldn't we be going down instead of up?"

"If the engine fails, I want to have a bigger cushion. This plane has a ten-to-one glide ratio."

"I have no idea what that means."

"Any plane can glide if the engine fails. The ratio is a comparison of the relative travel of a plane when it's in glide mode, flying without power. With this plane, it can move forward ten units for every single unit of altitude it loses. We are flying at eleven hundred feet, so if the engine stalled right now, we could travel eleven thousand feet forward before we hit the surface, and I'd like to have another five hundred feet or more."

The engine seemed to catch again, and the whole plane shuddered. I felt my whole body flush.

"That was it again, right?"

"Yes. There's a crop-dusting business with a small runway just past Henrietta. It's about forty-five miles from here."

"Aren't you afraid we'll be caught when we land?"

"That business closes for the night, but they can't close the runway. We can put down there, and our arrival won't be known until they find the plane when they open in the morning. We should have at least two hours to get away."

Basically, any plan that involved us being on the ground seemed like a good idea.

The plane shuddered again, and there was silence. My heart rose up into my throat. I looked out. The propeller wasn't spinning, just slowly turning in the breeze.

"Gene?"

"I'm trying to restart the engine."

I became aware of the sound of rushing air and felt the sensation of us going down. Gene worked the controls. I stared at the propeller, trying to will it back to life.

"You need to make sure your seatbelt is tight," Gene said. "I'm going to put us down on the highway."

That made sense. It wasn't far, and what was the difference between a road and a runway? Except the interstate had cars and trucks and big rigs. I realized that there were only a couple of sets of lights along the entire stretch of highway I could see. We could probably land between those vehicles and get out of the plane before something came along and hit us. But what then?

How long would it take before somebody called the police or

a police car just came along? It could only be a few minutes —
fifteen or twenty at the most. But what choice did we have?

I looked below. The sun was just starting to come up over the
horizon, and I was able to make out the shadows below. It was a
field, and it looked flat. We could always land there if we couldn't
make the highway. Maybe we shouldn't even try for the interstate.

"Could you put us down in the field instead?" I asked.

"Landing on the highway increases our chance of a successful
landing."

"But doesn't it also increase the chances of us being unsuc-
cessful after we land?" I asked.

"I'm not following."

"A highway landing is going to get everybody's attention, including calls for the police. How far could we get before they arrived?"
I asked.

"You're right. I just hadn't thought of that."

"Hard to believe I out-thought you."

"There are many ways that you're smarter. I have great quantities of information, but information isn't necessarily knowledge,
and knowledge isn't wisdom."

I couldn't help but laugh. "That sounds like wisdom to me."

"I just read it. That's all. It's like back in my room. You knew
that operative had gotten himself untied, and I didn't notice."

"There was something about his expression, the way he was,
well, holding himself," I said.

"Neither of which I noticed. I have more information than
you, but often you have more wisdom than me."

"Maybe it would be wise if you focused on flying instead of
this discussion. Please."

He nodded. "Yes, of course." He was looking out the side window at the ground beneath us. I knew he was studying it.

"Do you think you can land us in the field?"

"It's very flat. I should be able to. I'm going to try."

Gene adjusted course, and as he turned, the plane seemed to slow and drop even faster. The ground was coming up at us quickly. He leveled out, and the descent slowed.

"You can do this, right?"

"I studied all the emergency procedures, including landing with a stalled engine. I'm prepared for this. We're lucky we're already flying into the wind so that I don't have to try to bring it around. It's always best to land into the wind."

"I guess that's reassuring."

"Even better — the rows in the fields are running in the same direction we're going to land. The ground is most likely to be level in the direction the rows are running because the farmer plants to minimize erosion and runoff of fertilizer."

"How do you know that?"

"I read the entire manual on emergency landings less than ten hours ago, remember? I'm the best prepared pilot in the country in crash procedures."

That was so reassuring in such a strange way.

We were now so low that the highway had disappeared from view. I knew it was somewhere over to the right, but I couldn't see it. And that meant that people driving on the highway couldn't see a plane setting down in the field.

Gene was fully absorbed with the controls. There was just the sound of the wind. I was terrified.

"Becky, I'm going to tell you exactly what I'm doing."

"You don't have to do that. I don't want to distract you."

"It won't distract me. It will help for me to talk it through. I will not just be thinking it, but hearing it."

"Two different methods of retrieval and processing," I said.

"Exactly," he confirmed. "I'm going to be aiming for the top of the corn. In my calculations, it's the floor rather than the ground beneath it."

"I don't know what that means, but sure, go ahead," I said.

"All airplanes have what they call a stall speed. That's the speed where you stop going forward and start going down. I'm going to try to reach stall speed just above the top of the stalks. The stalks will slow us down and act as cushioning as we crash and —"

"Could we call it a landing instead of a crash?"

"It's a crash landing. No lies, remember."

The stalks were coming up so quickly.

"I want you to reach down and take the handle of your door and slightly open it."

"What?"

"We do that in case the impact jams the doors. I'm doing the same. Don't worry. The push of the air will keep it closed, and your belt will hold you in place."

I fumbled around and found the handle. I pushed it down. It clicked, and I could hear the wind swooshing through a little gap that had opened up.

We were getting lower and lower.

"I'm going to be pulling the plane's nose. As I do that, you'll feel a further slowdown. The slower the speed, the less the impact."

The front of the plane tipped up, and the stalks disappeared.

"Here we go."

Instantly I could hear the bottom of the plane plowing through the tops of the corn, and then cornstalks started crashing against the windshield. I went to scream, but my breath was pushed out by the seatbelt crushing me as I surged forward. The wheels hit the ground, and we bounced and bounced. The plane tipped violently to one side, the wing on my side dipping down. For a second it felt like we were going to flip over, and then we leveled off and stopped.

33

THERE WAS COMPLETE silence. The windshield was covered with cornstalks, and I looked down at the dashboard. A large crack snaked up the console.

"Are you all right?" Gene asked as he reached out and placed a hand on my shoulder.

"Better than I thought I'd be. You?"

"Fine. We'd better get out in case there's a fire."

I didn't see any smoke, but I felt another rush of panic. I fumbled with my seatbelt, hit the release button in the center, and the pieces all came open. I tried the door, but it didn't want to open. We'd sunk slightly into the ground, and one of the furrows was pressed against it. I turned and used both legs to shove, and it flew open. I jumped to the ground beside the plane. My whole body felt like it was buzzing, like there was electricity flowing through it.

"Here, take these," Gene said.

I took the two packs that Gene had grabbed from the back. They felt incredibly heavy — heavier than usual — and I realized it wasn't them, it was me. I felt weak. My legs were wobbly, and I was shaking.

Gene climbed out his side of the plane carrying the precious briefcase. He circled behind the plane. Behind us were two deep ruts where the wheels had finally touched down and had created a path of broken and beaten-down corn. Beyond that, the stalks rose so high that I couldn't see past them. We, and the plane, were hidden.

The shaking in my legs got worse; my stomach heaved, and I felt like I was going to throw up. I bent over and tried to breathe, but my chest felt so tight.

"Just try to take a deep breath." He put a hand on my back and started to rub it.

I nodded. "We just walked away from a plane crash," I whispered.

"It's hard. I understand," Gene said.

"But we did walk away. That makes this a good landing, so why am I shaking?" I asked.

"Your body filled with adrenaline to prepare for that, and now it's surging through you and you're having a normal physiological reaction."

"You're not having it," I said, trying to focus on my breath as I talked.

"I think we've established I'm many things. Normal isn't one of them. I am a little surprised by it all, though. Usually, people don't simply walk away from a plane crash without some form of injury."

"We had a good pilot."

"We had a lucky pilot," Gene said.

"My father always says that sometimes being lucky is better than being good."

"Good has been what I've always aimed for. Did you know that it's nineteen times more dangerous to fly in a small private plane than it is to drive in a car?"

"I'm glad I didn't know that until now."

"I thought it best to save that piece of information until we landed."

Gene cleared away some of the stalks that covered the engine of the plane. There was a series of holes. "This is where the bullets hit. We were lucky the damage didn't end our flight immediately. I think a bullet might have nicked the gas line, and eventually we just ran out of gas. Are you ready to go? Do you think you can walk?"

"I can run if I have to."

"Before we landed, I saw there was a barn and an old house a few hundred yards in front of us. Let's head that way," Gene suggested. He threw one of the packs over his shoulder and gave me the second. He had the briefcase in one hand and took my hand with the other.

We started walking, and there, just in front of us, no more than two dozen feet ahead, was a metal fence strung along between wooden posts. I walked over and placed a hand against it. On the other side of the fence was a drainage ditch that dipped down three or four feet.

"What would have happened if we'd hit that fence?" I asked.

"It probably would have shattered the front of the plane, maybe broken our legs, and splinters and pieces would have been thrown through the windshield and caused upper body trauma or possible death or —"

"I think I get it. We were lucky."

"Lucky."

We climbed the fence and went down the drainage ditch — there was a little bit of water at the bottom — and then up the other side. We moved through the corn until we came to a gravel driveway and turned to the left toward the farmhouse. The gravel crunching under my feet felt good.

The driveway opened up to a large yard. There was a house to the right and a big barn to the left. Both had peeling paint and looked like they'd seen far better days. Off to the side was an old, beaten-up pickup truck. Probably every farm in the country had an old pickup truck. We walked up onto the porch, and Gene knocked on the door. There was no answer. He raised his hand to knock again when a voice came from inside.

"I'm coming, I'm coming!" It was a gruff, older-sounding male voice.

The door was thrown open, and an old man appeared. He was in worn clothes and had a scruffy gray beard and messy, longish hair. One of his eyes looked all hazy.

"Sorry to bother you, sir," I said.

He turned his head to the side so the one good eye was facing us. He leaned and looked around us. "I don't see no car."

"Our car broke down on the interstate," Gene said.

"And you wandered off the highway instead of staying there with your car?" he asked.

"We thought you might have a phone we could use."

"Are you the only two kids in the world who don't own cellphones?"

That was a good question. One Gene wasn't going to be able to answer.

"We have phones, but they were both out of power," I quickly explained. "Could we get a ride or use your phone to call for a ride to the nearest town?"

"Can't give you a ride. Government took away my license 'cause they said I was half blind, but I can call you a tow truck or a taxi. You both probably need a coffee."

He retreated back inside, and the screen door closed with a big thud.

"I could *really* use a coffee," I said to Gene.

We entered the farmhouse. The hall was long and dim, and the place smelled musty. We moved toward the light at the far end of the corridor. The old man was standing by the stove and looked over his shoulder as we came into the room.

"Take a seat," he said, gesturing to the table.

I went to sit down and stopped myself. I could see a television on in the other room. The volume was too low to hear, but it was on one of the cable news stations. I looked at Gene, and he nodded at me; he'd noticed too. It was a commercial, but there was no question that if the man had been watching the channel at all, he would have seen us at some point. That is, if his eyesight was good enough to see us on TV or to see us now and put the two together.

We took a seat at the table.

"What do you take in your coffee?" the man asked.

"Black for both of us, sir," I answered.

Gene drank coffee now. When he'd first started, I'd thought

he was just doing it to fit in. Now he seemed to really crave the caffeine.

"Black is the best way to take coffee. I don't understand people who put things in to cover up the real taste of the bean. Pumpkin flavored, full of sprinkles and steamed milk and soy crap. That's not a coffee, it's some hipster, yuppie invention."

He brought over two steaming mugs of coffee. It smelled so good that the mugs being stained and chipped didn't matter. As he put them down, I noticed how shaky his hands were.

"Thank you," I said.

"Yes, thank you, sir," Gene said.

"You two got good manners."

"Just the way we were raised," I said.

"Are you brother and sister?"

I laughed. "Boyfriend and girlfriend. We just both have parents who told us to show manners to older people."

"Then you should be *really* respectful to me, 'cause I'm *really* old."

He laughed at his own joke as he went back over to the stove and poured himself a cup as well.

"Where were you headed before your car broke down?"

"We're driving to Upstate New York," I said.

"It's a big state. Whereabouts are you heading?"

I wanted to change the subject. "This is about the best cup of coffee I've ever had."

"Better than that Starbucks place and at about a tenth of the price. You sure you never been to one of those Starbucks places?"

"No, sir, there isn't one where we live."

"You sound like you're born and raised in the Midwest. My guess is Indiana."

I was surprised he could tell, but I wasn't going to tell him exactly where I was from. "Yes, a place called Arcade."

"That's not far from Nobleton, right?" he asked.

Him saying that unnerved me. Gene and I exchanged a look. "Not far," I admitted. "Do you live here alone?" I asked, once more trying to redirect him.

"Me and my son. He's gone to work for the day, but he was born and raised right here. How about you, Becky? Were you born and raised in Indiana?"

"Yes, sir. So were my parents and my ... how did you know my name?"

"Um, you told me. Becky and Gene, right?"

"No, we didn't tell you our names, and you didn't tell us yours," Gene said.

"Heck, that was rude of me. I'm Henry." He reached behind his back and pulled out a revolver and pointed it at us. "And this is my gun, and it doesn't have a name."

34

"YOU DON'T WANT to be making any sudden moves," he said.

I didn't think I could make any moves, sudden or not. I was frozen in fear.

"I suppose it wouldn't help to say that you have the wrong people," Gene guessed.

"I'm half blind, not half stupid."

"I'm sorry if my statement implied that, sir."

Henry chuckled. "Still polite even when a gun is pointed at you. Your parents did raise you right, at least before you killed them."

"He didn't kill them!" I exclaimed.

"Was it you, then?"

"Of course not!"

"Are you gonna try to convince me you're nothing but his hostage?" Henry asked.

I shook my head. "I'm here because he's my boyfriend and we had no choice."

"Like they said on the TV. You two is either Romeo and Juliet or Bonnie and Clyde."

"We're not Bonnie and Clyde. We didn't do anything wrong."

"That's not what they're saying on the TV. Doesn't matter if it's Fox News or CNN, every time I turn on the set, there you are."

I turned and looked at the television. It showed the same two photos that I'd seen before. The picture was fuzzy, but we were unmistakable.

"What happens now?" Gene asked.

"We wait for my son to come this afternoon. Guess I didn't mention that I don't really have a phone for you to call anybody."

"And what happens when your son comes?" Gene asked.

"We cart you off to the police station."

"If you do that, we're dead," I said.

"No matter what you done or didn't do, even if you were found guilty there isn't no death penalty in New York."

"We'll never see a court. We'll never make it that far. We'll be killed," I said. "At least, I'll be killed, and Gene will disappear."

"I've known Sheriff Paul Watson my whole life, and he'll make sure you're safe and cared for. He's a good man."

"He's going to be dead, too. He and all his deputies. It's not just me they're going to kill when they take Gene."

"Go on," he said.

That surprised me. "What's the point? It's not like you're going to believe me."

"Why not keep talking? It's not like you got anyplace to go or anything to do."

I looked at Gene for guidance. He nodded, giving me approval.

"I'm just impressed that the two of you managed to get this far without being caught. Did you steal the car that broke down?"

"We did take a truck," I said. "But we left that in Indiana, in a cornfield."

"Then how did you get here?"

"By plane, but we didn't steal it as much as borrow it."

"Borrowed it?" he asked.

"We left money behind. We did the same for the truck we took."

"If you came by plane, where's the plane?"

"In your neighbor's cornfield. We had to make an emergency landing."

"You two seem to like leaving things in cornfields," he said.

I couldn't help but chuckle.

"And you walked away? What happened to the pilot? Did you kill him, too?"

"He's sitting here," I said, pointing at Gene.

"You can fly a plane?"

He nodded.

"Figure they would have mentioned that in the news."

"Yesterday Gene didn't know how to fly," I answered.

He looked confused. It was confusing to anybody who didn't know the truth about Gene.

"Gene, can I tell him more?"

Again, he nodded.

"Gene can learn things faster than any other human being because he's different from anybody else on the planet."

"Are you saying he's some form of alien?"

"Not an alien. Just different. He didn't know how to fly a plane when we left, but he learned so we could take the plane."

"Obviously didn't learn that well or you wouldn't have had to land in a cornfield."

"We think the plane was damaged when we were shot at during takeoff."

"Who shot at you?"

"We're not sure. They were shooting at us from their SUVs.

It could have been the same people who killed his parents, who tried to capture Gene."

"Then you saw them, right?"

"They had guns on us. They threatened to kill him if we didn't turn over the serum."

"Serum? What's that?"

I had said too much, and I knew it. I had no choice but to go on. "It's something Gene takes to help him learn things fast."

"Is it like a drug?"

"No," Gene said. "It's a naturally occurring enzyme. It's been isolated, extracted, and concentrated to make it more effective."

"And except for the vial Gene took to learn to fly, we destroyed it all before we ran," I said.

He didn't need to know about the three and a half vials still in the briefcase. At least, we didn't need to tell him.

"And you take this stuff and you can learn how to fly a plane?"

"Like Becky said, I took the last dose we had so I could learn that."

"And these men who had guns on you, how many of them were there?" he asked.

"Two who came into the house, but we think another four outside the house. Somebody was jamming our cellphones so we couldn't call anybody."

"Is that why you don't have cellphones, because you tossed them away?"

"We turned them off and put them in packs with lead shielding," Gene said.

"Smart," Henry said. "They can be used to track your position and even have their microphones and cameras turned on like a bugging device."

Those were things Gene had said. "How do you know all of that?" I asked.

"I read. I listen. Reason I don't have any phone is I don't want nobody invading my privacy. Those men, they're the ones who killed your parents?"

"Yes. They weren't really my parents," Gene said. "They were scientists assigned to the project."

Henry nodded. His reactions — words and expressions — weren't what I'd expected. Did he actually believe what we were saying?

"And the men chasing you, were they dressed all in black?" he asked.

Him saying that had to mean something. "How did you know that?" I asked.

"That's the way they always dress," he answered. "White shirts, black suits with matching shoes and belt, and dark sunglasses."

They had been in tracksuits.

"It's like you were there," I said, humoring him. "That's exactly how they dressed."

"When you took the plane, you turned off the transponder, right?" he asked.

"Yes," Gene replied.

"And you flew low to try to avoid radar?"

"We stayed under four hundred feet for most of the time until after we were out of the range of the Buffalo Niagara International Airport."

"Good. That only leaves satellite imagery."

Before I could think to ask, he gave the answer.

"I know lots of things. Do you know that every major city in the world has a drone in constant flight that takes a picture every thirty seconds?"

"I didn't, but why would they do that?"

"Constant video surveillance," he explained.

"Are you sure about that?" I asked.

"He's right," Gene confirmed. "Then they have a continuous record of activity in the city."

"But why would they want that?"

"It was originally used by the U.S. military in Iraq to combat roadside bombings," Gene explained.

"A bomb would explode, and they would go back through the images," Henry added. "They would find the vehicle or people who planted it and look through the time-lapse images to find where they went so they could neutralize them."

I looked at Gene once more, and he nodded.

"Henry, your knowledge of that is particularly surprising. That's top-level, ultra-secret information," Gene said.

"A better question is, how do you know how secret they are?" Henry asked in reply.

This next answer was important. It might be better if it was a question instead.

"What do you think?" I asked.

"I'm not sure what to think, but it might be the ways I learn. Me, I'm an old man with lots of time on my hands. I learn things a lot of different ways. The dark net, blogs, podcasts, chatrooms, alternate news sites, and even cable news all provide information."

"Go on," I said. I figured he didn't need much encouragement to keep talking. Maybe we could distract him, and Gene could get the gun off of him.

"You have to understand that cable news is something the real people in power use to put out what they call false narratives. They tell you what they want you to know. So, you figure you understand the world when you understand nothing."

"Fake news?"

"Not fake, just distorted. You have to know how to watch it."

"I don't understand."

"It's like reading the negative in a picture. You have to look at the parts they *don't* say to know what's *really* happening."

"And you understand?"

"I understand a lot more than most," he said.

His voice had softened, and the gun was aimed more at the ground than at us.

Everything he was saying sounded unbelievable. I'd heard about people like him — conspiracy theorists. Disgruntled people who believed almost anything no matter how bizarre. But was what he was saying any more unbelievable than anything that had happened to us in the last seventy-two hours?

"You know what all of this means?" Henry asked.

I had no idea. I didn't even have an idea of an idea.

"You two better get going," he said.

"What?"

He put down his coffee on the stove and spun the gun around so he was holding it by the barrel. "It won't be long until they track you this far."

He limped across the room and handed the gun to Gene.

35

MY MIND SPUN, trying to understand what was happening. "You're not holding us prisoner?"

"Giving him the gun would be a pretty stupid way to do that."

Gene had taken the gun and placed it on the table beside him.

"You have to leave, and the sooner the better," Henry continued.

"But you said your son isn't going to be home until this afternoon," I said.

"It's not my son I'm worried about. It won't be long until they track you here. That plane isn't invisible from the sky."

"Satellites and drones," I said, almost thinking out loud.

"Exactly. Do you know they can read your license plate from space?" Henry asked. "And that's why you have to leave right away before they get here."

He was wrong about so much, but he was right about that. We had to leave quickly — but what about him?

"You should come with us so you'll be safe."

"I have another plan. We'll knock over a couple of chairs, maybe smash a couple of plates so it looks like you overpowered me. I'm going to need you to handcuff me so that nobody comes after me for helping you."

Gene didn't miss a beat. "You have handcuffs?"

"Third drawer down 'side the fridge."

"I'll get them," I said.

I walked across the room and opened the drawer. There were two pairs of handcuffs, some big hunting knives, and what looked like cans of pepper spray — and was that a taser? I fished out both pairs of handcuffs. The keys were in the locks already.

"Do you want me to put them on you?"

"Not yet. Just put 'em on the table. I'll lock myself up a few hours from now when I hear somebody coming, whether it's those people chasing you or my son."

"You're going to hide this from your son as well?" I asked.

"Best to protect him by keeping him in the dark." He chuckled. "Besides, he won't believe any of it. He already thinks I'm something between paranoid and crazy."

I put the cuffs on the table.

"Thank you for helping us," Gene said.

"I ain't going to help the dark forces."

"I'm just glad you believe what we told you," I added.

"Everything you told me was true, wasn't it?"

"Of course. You have to admit, it just seems so unbelievable," I said.

"That's what makes it so believable. Not just what you told me, but what's on the news."

"The news says Gene's a killer and I'm his hostage."

"*All* the news says that," Henry said. "Not just CNN and MSNBC but also Fox News. They all say the same thing exactly."

"Isn't that even more reason that you shouldn't believe us?"

"That's what you got wrong. They hardly never agree on nothing. The fact that they agree on your story means the real powers that control things want the world to believe your boyfriend is a killer to hide what really happened."

What he was saying seemed to make sense.

"You'll take my truck. It's old, but it works. The keys are inside." He turned to Gene. "Do you drive any better than you fly?"

"I'm going to drive." I hesitated and then told him the rest. "Gene doesn't know how to drive a car."

Henry burst into laughter. It was all scratchy and growly.

"Isn't that a kick in the head! You can fly a plane, but you can't drive a car. Anyway, when you're through with my truck you can push it off a cliff so that the insurance company has to buy it out."

"We want to pay you for it." Gene opened up his pack and removed a wad of bills. "How much do you think it's worth?"

"You don't seem to understand the idea of *stealing*. If you leave me with money, they'll know I was cooperating. I was thinking that maybe you should even slap me around a little to make it look like a fight."

"We can't do that!" I protested.

"Suit yourself, but put away that money."

Gene put the bills back inside his pack.

My eye was caught by a big "BREAKING NEWS" banner across the screen of the television in the other room. There was a dark, grainy video of a plane taxiing down a runway with three big, black SUVs in pursuit. They were all coming toward the surveillance camera. There was a flash of light from one of the vehicles, and then a second and third and fourth, and then the plane and the SUVs went out of the camera's view.

"Where's the volume? Where's the remote?" I demanded.

I raced into the living room, and Gene and Henry followed

behind. The remote was on the arm of a green reclining chair. I turned up the sound.

"That surveillance video shows shots being fired as three unknown vehicles chase a plane as it is being stolen," the announcer said.

The same footage came on again. Even though I knew we were in that plane, it was hard to comprehend that I was part of the images I was seeing.

"The police believe the plane was stolen as part of a drug smuggling operation that went bad between rival drug gangs," he continued.

"They don't know it was us," I said.

"They know," Henry said. "They just don't want the world to know. That footage is hard to explain if it's just men in black firing their guns and chasing you."

"It appears that Indiana has become quite the hot spot in the last few days as we return to our other lead story," the announcer said.

Once again, our pictures were flashed up on the screen behind his head, and he talked about our continued ability to avoid arrest. I clicked the set off. No point in watching any more.

"You better get going," Henry said. "Won't be long till the plane is tracked to here. The truck's tank is half full."

"We don't have too far —"

"No, don't tell me!" he exclaimed, cutting Gene off. "Better I don't know. Less that can be interrogated or tortured or drugged out of me. Enough talk; you have to get going."

I TURNED THE key, and the engine coughed and sputtered but wouldn't catch. A getaway car that wouldn't get away wasn't much good.

"Don't go flooding it," Henry said.

I turned the key again, and it whirred without result.

"How long has it been since you've used this truck?" I asked.

"Two months at most."

I turned the key again, and it started. I revved the engine. It was loud, and the whole truck rumbled. I caught sight of a haze of blue exhaust smoke in the rearview mirror.

"I told you she'd work."

Gene leaned across the seat and reached out, and the two shook hands. "Thanks for everything, Henry."

"My pleasure. Not every day you get to defeat the dark forces. You two better get driving. You have at least five hours till my son is back, so the truck won't be reported stolen until then."

"And if the men in black get here first?" Gene asked.

"They'll find an addled old man, handcuffed, who don't know nothing, including the color or type of truck that he owns. Now, get going; if they were tracking your plane by satellite, they might not be far behind you."

"Thank you for everything," I said.

"Least I could do. If I was a few years younger, I'd come along and help out. Speaking of which, you better take this."

He reached behind his back and took out his gun. For a split second I thought he was pulling it on us again, but he handed it to Gene.

"You should keep it," I said.

"You might need it. Besides, it would be hard to explain why you took my gun from me and left it behind. You take care of him," he said to me.

"We take care of each other," I replied.

"I get that, but I figure he might be the one with all those brains, but you're the one with all the smarts. Keep him safe."

"I will. I promise," I said.

"Now, get going so I can go inside and settle in and wait for 'em to arrive."

I put the truck into gear, and we started away. I looked in the rearview mirror and saw Henry standing in the cloud of dust we were leaving, waving goodbye. We bumped along the lane until we came to the interstate. We came up to a ditch that separated us from the pavement. I slowed and angled us down the embankment, and the bottom of the truck scraped as we started up the other side. I tried to signal, but the indicator didn't work, then I looked in my sideview mirror and entered the lane. As I accelerated, the truck began shaking and rattling.

"I wish we could have stolen a better truck," I said.

"Better trucks might have come with people less likely to let us have them."

"A few days ago, I would have thought everything he said was crazy."

"A lot of it *is* false. Men in black suits is a thing conspiracy theorists talk about all the time, but really, if you're trying to stay unseen, should you all wear the same black suit?"

"You're right, tracksuits do fit in better sometimes."

"But you agreed with him and said our attackers were wearing black suits," Gene said.

"I thought agreeing with him would help convince him."

"I wouldn't have thought of that."

"Like Henry said, sometimes I'm the smart one." I paused. "But he was right about other things, like the dark net, drones, and the satellites. Those are things you've talked about."

"Those are real. Other things are just wild conspiracy theories." Gene shrugged. "Then again, who would think I'm real?"

"I wouldn't have believed any of it. How do you know all of these things?"

"You give a teenager with my intellectual abilities unlimited access to powerful supercomputers and time to explore and you can find almost anything."

"And how many people know all of these things?"

"There are so many levels. I wonder how many more there are that even I don't know anything about. Right now, I just can't think about it. I'm tired. More tired than I ever remember being."

"You should be tired. I slept last night, but you were piloting the plane. Why don't you go to sleep?"

"I'm not sure if I should."

"Just put your head down and close your eyes for a bit."

"I guess I could do that. You'll wake me if there's a problem, right?"

"Oh, believe me, I'll wake you. How far do I go along the Thruway?"

"It's still a long way from here. Go until you reach Albany. Take Highway 87 north toward Lake Placid. It's just a few exits past there, but I'll be awake long before that."

He curled up on the bench. He looked cramped with his knees up almost at his chin.

"Scrunch over a bit; use me as your pillow."

He put his head on my lap. I reached down and put a hand on his head and gently stroked his hair.

"That feels so good. Thank you … thanks for everything. I'm sorry for getting you into this. For putting your life in danger."

"It's not like it's just my life. We're in this together, the two of us."

"I never thought I'd have a together. I always thought it would just be me, one of a kind … no match … no partner … alone."

"You're not alone."

"Thank you. I really was made for you."

"Go to sleep. And remember, I love you."

36

THE LAKE PLACID exit was coming up. Gene had been asleep for almost three hours. At times, his nose whistled in his sleep. The noise was reassuring, reminding me he was there. On three separate occasions, we'd passed a police car that had either stopped somebody for speeding or was driving in the other direction. I was pretty sure there hadn't been word put out that the truck had been stolen, but if I was a police officer, I might have pulled this bucket of bolts over for a safety check.

"Gene," I said softly. "It's time to get up."

Gene's eyes popped open, and he sat up. "Where are we?"

"Lake Placid is the next exit."

"I can't believe I slept that long. Were there any problems?"

"A car chase, a Black Hawk helicopter, a couple of drones, a few ninjas, a dozen men in black suits, and some robots. Nothing I couldn't handle. How much farther?"

"It's less than a twenty-minute drive."

"We're going to make it," I said as I kept driving.

Gene gave me a smile.

I slowed down and eased into the exit lane for Plattsburgh. I made the turn, and there, right in front of me blocking the road, was a police car. There was an officer standing in front of the car. I put on the brakes, and we skidded to a stop no more than a dozen feet in front of her. I went to throw the truck into reverse when a second police car came out of the ditch and slid in behind me, pinning me in. We were trapped!

"We have to run for it," Gene said. "Out my door and into the woods."

We did have a gun. It had slid off the seat and onto the floor. Maybe it was our only chance. But I couldn't use a gun on anyone, let alone a cop.

"Gene … Becky!" The officer to the front had a radio microphone in her hand, and she was using the speaker system of the squad car. "You don't have to run … you can go home!" she called out. "The people who killed your parents have been caught!"

"Gene, do you hear what she's saying?"

"I hear her."

The officer had walked away from her car toward us. She had her hands in the air. "Look, no guns!"

The other officer did the same, and his hands were also in front of him, his gun still in the holster.

I rolled down the window, and she came right up to the side of the truck.

"Word came down. We know you didn't kill anybody. We know you were just running for your lives. You're safe now," the officer said.

Both of them were smiling. I had such a rush of relief I had to stop myself from bursting into tears.

"It's over," I said to Gene.

We climbed out of the truck. Gene had the briefcase in his hand. The male officer gave Gene a slap on the back as the pair introduced themselves as Greg and Gina.

"You two must have somebody up high who likes you," Officer Gina said.

"Yeah, word came down from the top. We're just glad that this could happen without anybody getting hurt," Officer Greg said.

"I'll pull your truck off to the side," Officer Gina said.

"I can do that."

"No need. Are the keys inside?"

"Yes."

"Come on over, have a seat. You must be exhausted," the male officer said.

He led us over to his car as the other officer first moved her squad car so that our truck could be freed enough to be moved as well.

"You two must really have a story to tell," he said. "Managing to steal a plane is pretty unbelievable," he said.

"You know about the plane?" I asked.

"We know about everything. Pretty impressive that you got this far."

The officer had moved the squad car to the side and climbed into our truck to do the same. For some reason, I didn't like her in there, in our truck, in Henry's truck.

"What's in that case?" the officer asked as he tapped a finger against the briefcase.

"Nothing special," Gene said.

"Sure looks special the way you're guarding it, but what do I know? I'm just a state trooper."

"Could you do one thing?" Gene asked. "Can you just radio in that we're fine and have somebody call Becky's parents?"

"They'll know soon enough."

"Please, it would mean so much if you could," I added.

The officer circled around the side of the car. I noticed he was keeping an eye on us as he sat down and pulled out the microphone from the radio. And then I saw something.

I pulled Gene closer, wrapping my arms around him, and whispered in his ear. "The policeman is wearing a Rolex watch. It's worth ten thousand dollars."

"How can a policeman afford —"

"He can't," I whispered. "No policeman could. I don't think they're police."

"You have to get away with the serum. I'm going to give you a chance to get away. Dump the serum as soon as you can and get lost in the woods."

"I can't just leave you."

"You have to. Don't even look back. Just run."

He released me before I had a chance to argue.

The officer was off the radio and came back to our side. "Your parents are being called as we speak," he said cheerfully. And so believably. I knew he hadn't called anybody.

I glanced at his hands. I couldn't see the watch beneath his sleeve. I turned around as the female officer joined us. Her uniform fit so badly, and her shoes were all wrong. Instead of standard black dress shoes, they were much dressier. They were as wrong as that Rolex on the other guy's wrist. We had to get away.

If I could make an excuse to go back to the truck, I could grab the gun from the floor if she hadn't taken it already.

"I hope you don't mind riding in the back," Officer Gina said as she opened the back door of the squad car. "It's police procedure."

"Not at all," Gene said. "Probably safer back there anyway. Could you do one more thing, please? You were right. There really is something so valuable in this briefcase that people are willing to kill for it. I don't want to even have it in my hands anymore. Could one of you take it?"

"Of course, no problem!" Officer Greg said.

He came forward and reached out his hand, and Gene kicked him between the legs. As the officer doubled over, Gene brought the briefcase up and slammed him in the face, causing him to fly backward. The other officer grabbed for her gun, and Gene hit her in the side of the head with the briefcase, knocking her over.

"Run!" Gene screamed as he tossed me the briefcase and then jumped on top of Officer Gina on the ground.

I ran two steps and stopped. Officer Greg was still on the ground, stunned, struggling to sit up. If he got his gun out, he could shoot me or Gene. I had to get away — no, we'd come too far together for that. I rushed over and swung the briefcase upward, hitting the officer under the chin with full force. The impact made a sickening sound, and his head snapped back. He tumbled backward, and his head smacked against the ground with an even louder thud. His jaw was on an awkward angle, his scalp was cut and blood was flowing, his eyes were open but unfocused. I reached down and tried to grab his gun from the holster. I fumbled with the clip that was holding it in place for a few seconds until it came free. I turned. Gene was struggling with the woman.

"Stop, now!" I yelled as I pointed the gun.

The fight went on. I couldn't shoot at her without risking hitting Gene. In one motion, she flipped Gene over then grabbed him from behind, and a knife appeared in her hand at Gene's throat.

"Drop the gun!" she yelled to me.

I lowered it.

"No," Gene said. "Don't drop the gun!"

"Shut up!" she yelled. "Either you drop the gun or he's dead."

"If you drop the gun, we're both dead," Gene said.

"I told you to shut up!"

"The only way you can shut me up is to kill me," Gene said. "Becky, if you give her the gun, she'll kill you and then take me, and I'll be as good as dead. Shoot her. If you hit me instead it doesn't matter. Just make sure you keep shooting until she's dead."

I brought the gun up and aimed directly at them — at her head.

"Are you willing to risk killing your boyfriend?" she asked.

"Yes," I answered. I was trying to sound calm and confident. "Because Gene's right. I have no choice." Then I thought of something. "For you this is just about the money, right?"

"A lot of money," she replied.

"We have money. There's a fortune in our escape bags. We can leave it for you."

She didn't respond. She was thinking. "How much?"

"Almost two hundred thousand dollars," I lied, exaggerating the amount we were carrying. "We'll leave the bag in the woods. Just over there. You can come back later and get it. You won't even have to split it with your partner."

He was lying unconscious.

"Assuming he's alive," I said. "We'll handcuff you and leave."

"And how do I know you'll actually leave the money?" she asked.

"You know we didn't kill the other two operatives back at Gene's house," I said. "We left them tied up in his room. We're not killers. We just want to get away, and you just want the money. Everybody wins and nobody dies." I paused. "Not even you."

She nodded her head ever so slightly. She dropped the knife and released Gene, who, in one motion, scooped up the knife and got to his feet. He turned around and took the gun from the woman's holster.

I heard the sound of a car and spun around, terrified it could be more of them. It wasn't. It was an older car, and in it were two even older people, a man and a woman. I quickly lowered the gun and meekly waved at them, and the woman waved back as they slowly drove onto the shoulder of the road, managing to just squeeze by the squad car and drive away. Had they seen me holding the gun, pointing it at the officer, or the other officer lying on the ground? Had they figured out what was happening, or had they thought it was something more innocent?

Gene took the cuffs from the officer's belt and walked her over to the patrol car parked off to the side. He put one cuff on her wrist and slapped the second on the door handle of the car. He went back to the first operative, who was still unconscious, took his cuffs, then flipped him over and cuffed his hands behind his back. Gene walked over to me and took the gun. I was relieved to be rid of it.

"I have a question for you," Gene said to the woman. "These cars, the uniforms, where did you get them from?"

"Where do you think?"

"I think you killed two officers and took their cars and uniforms."

She shrugged. "It was necessary. Of course, the media is going to believe they were two more victims of your murder spree."

"How did you know to be here, to block this road?"

"We have agents in place in dozens and dozens of spots surrounding the whole Plattsburgh area."

"But how did you know to look here?"

She shrugged. "I just follow orders. I don't know where the intel came from."

I did. "It was from me," I said. "When I thought that man who broke in to your house was a scout at the basketball game, I told him that you used to live near Plattsburgh. It's my fault."

"You didn't know. You couldn't have known," Gene said.

"Where are you going to leave the money? Make sure it's far enough from the road that nobody will see it."

"That's not a problem," Gene said. "We're not leaving you anything."

"But we had a deal!"

"I don't make deals with people like you." Gene raised the gun and aimed it toward her.

37

I CLOSED MY eyes as Gene fired the gun. I couldn't watch him kill somebody. He fired again, and then a third time. When I summoned the courage to open my eyes again, I saw he had shot the tires out of the squad car the woman was handcuffed to.

"Take the briefcase and get into the other squad car while I get our packs!" Gene ordered.

I unfroze and jumped in behind the wheel. The keys were in the ignition. I started the car as Gene, carrying the backpacks, climbed in beside me. The woman was violently pulling on the cuffs and kicking at the door of the other car trying to get free.

I threw the police car into gear and pushed down on the gas pedal, and the car squealed away, leaving a trail of rubber and a cloud of dust behind. We fishtailed as the car struggled to get traction before grabbing on to the asphalt.

"Be more careful, or I'll have to drive," Gene said.

"The last time you were behind the wheel of something we ended up crashing in a cornfield!"

"That was my bad attempt at a joke."

"You are starting to get this humor stuff. Did you really want me to shoot her ... to shoot toward you?"

"I wanted you to shoot her instead of me, but if you had to shoot me to do it, then, yes. I needed you to live."

The police radio jumped to life and startled me. It blared a request for the nearest squad car to investigate a "situation" at the Plattsburgh highway exit. That older couple must have seen enough to be concerned and called it in. It wouldn't be long until it was discovered and —

"I have to warn them!" Gene said.

"Warn them about what?"

"When the police arrive at the scene, they're going to think those are real officers in handcuffs and release them. Those operatives will kill them, take the new car, and escape." Gene was bent over, studying the radio. "We have to call and explain it to them."

I'd been in a police car many times before — Liv's father took the squad car home and had driven us to school in it — and I'd watched him on the radio.

"Pick up the receiver. There's a button on the side. Push it in and they can hear you. Then, if you release it, we can hear them."

Gene grabbed it. "Hello, police people. Can you hear me?"

There was static. "This is a secure band, please leave this wavelength immediately!"

"You have to warn the officers. Those people at the scene at the highway exit are not police officers."

"This is your only warning. You are interfering with police business."

"This *is* police business. There are two people in uniform who are handcuffed at the scene. They are *not* real police officers, I repeat, *not* real police officers. They stole the uniforms when they murdered two officers and stole their cars."

More static but no response. "Who is this?"

"It doesn't matter. You know there are two cars that you haven't been able to reach. Those officers were killed by the people at the scene who are now dressed in their uniforms. Do you understand?"

"I hear you."

"They are trained killers. You have to take extreme care or they will kill your officers. Do not, I repeat, do not undo their hand-cuffs. Do you roger that?"

"Roger … but who is this?"

Gene put the microphone back in its holder and turned off the radio as the dispatcher repeated his question, cutting him off mid-sentence.

"Shouldn't we leave that on?" I suggested. "That way we can listen to what they're saying."

"Of course, that makes sense." Gene turned it back on, and there was a lightning exchange of calls and replies as different cars asked questions and were dispatched and coordinated.

We came up behind a big tanker truck, and I had to slow down dramatically. The road curved and twisted, and there was a solid yellow line and no way to see if it was clear to pass. I peeked out over the line and then tucked back in as another big truck whizzed by in a blur of sound and sight.

"Do you hear that?" Gene asked. "It's a siren."

I did hear something. Anxiously, I looked in my rearview, but there was nobody behind us as far as the last curve in the road.

Of course, Gene could hear things I couldn't hear the same way he could see things I couldn't see.

"It's coming toward us," Gene said. "Get in as close as you can to the truck, and maybe we can pass unseen."

I edged forward, closer and closer. The siren was getting louder. I inched forward until I was no more than a few feet behind the tanker. I was so close I could no longer see the mirrors of the cab and suspected he couldn't see me either. I had to hope I was just as invisible to oncoming traffic.

Almost instantly, a police car, siren wailing and lights flashing, went shooting past, racing away. The siren faded away, and I watched the blue and red lights flashing as the car kept going. For a moment I thought we'd eluded him. Then I saw brake lights flash in my rearview.

"He's seen us! He's coming back!" I yelled.

I had to get around the truck. I thought about Liv's father's car. Sometimes, just for fun, he'd put on the lights and siren to get us to school in the morning. I reached over and flicked a couple of buttons, and our lights started flashing and our siren blaring. The truck driver saw my lights and eased slightly over. I pushed hard on the accelerator, and we passed. We came up to a tight curve, and our wheels squealed as I felt us sliding sideways. I took my foot off the gas, and we regained traction as the road straightened out. Once again, I pushed down on the gas pedal.

In the rearview I could see nothing but the big tanker truck. I knew the squad car was coming, but it hadn't made the pass yet. And then the radio came to life. It was that police car reporting that he'd spotted us and was in pursuit and wanted the road blockaded ahead of us.

"What are we going to do?" I screamed.

"We're not going far. There's a dirt road. It's coming up soon on your right."

We took one curve and then another. I was cutting corners,

trying not to slow down. Still nothing in my rearview, but with the curves I couldn't see far. But that also meant they couldn't see us. If we could get to the dirt road before they could see us, we'd be in the clear. I turned off the siren and the lights. They were only going to hurt us now.

"Slow down and get ready to brake hard and turn. There it is!"

I braked and cranked the wheel as I saw the dirt road off to the right. It felt like we were going up on two wheels before settling down. We dipped and turned as we shot up a dirt road that was more like a path closed in on both side by trees and bushes.

"Stop and turn off the engine," Gene ordered after we'd gone a short distance.

I slammed on the brakes, and we slid to the side of the path and came to a stop. I turned the car off. Although I couldn't see the main road, I could hear the siren of the other car as it got louder and louder and then much quieter and faded away.

"He passed us by. He didn't see us make the turn. Start driving again. The compound is over a ridge to the left. We'll get as close as we can by car before we have to walk."

For the first few hundred yards, the path was relatively flat and wide. Then everything changed. There were rocks sticking out and a lot of potholes, and I had to slow down so that we were creeping at not much more than a fast walk as we bounced down the path. The trees closed in so we could barely fit through the branches.

"I don't think I can drive much farther along this."

"Keep going as long as you can. When the path branches, take the left."

"You know this trail?"

"I've spent my entire life around here. I often wandered the woods by myself or with a guard."

I came to a stop at the fork. The route to the left was even smaller and rougher and dropped steeply. I turned the wheel, and we started down the slope. This felt risky ... and I started chuckling.

"What's funny?" Gene asked.

"I was thinking that this is the *least* dangerous thing I've done in the last few days."

There was a loud thud as something hit the bottom of the car, and we rocked up and over it. I accelerated, and the engine roared, but we were no longer moving. We were hung up on a rock. My father would have been so angry if I'd done this to our minivan.

And then I thought about my father and my mother and what they must have been thinking, what they'd been going through over the last few days. I'd been so busy going through it myself I'd hardly given them a thought.

"This is it," I said as I turned off the engine.

Gene climbed out his door, and I tried to get out my side but couldn't. The door could open only a few inches as it was jammed against a couple of small trees. I slid across the seat, then maneuvered myself over the radio and the shotgun. How eerie.

Gene was now holding the briefcase. With his free arm, he reached out and took my hand. It was reassuring and made me feel safe — or at least safer.

"Do you know how happy this makes me, holding your hand?" he asked.

"Probably as happy as it makes me."

I grabbed both our packs and handed one to him, then we started walking along the path.

"When we arrive, there are going to be lots of questions," Gene said.

"I'll answer anything they want to ask."

"You don't understand. I want you to answer most of their questions with 'I don't know.'"

"What do you mean?"

"It's better if you don't let them know that you know about the serum or the brain scans or that you were part of the experiment."

"But why?"

"The less you know, the better. You don't want to give them any reason to stop you from going back home, back to your old life."

"But you won't be coming, will you?"

He shook his head.

I'd been so focused on trying to stay alive that I hadn't even thought of what would happen when we got here. But really, had I thought Gene was going to go back to playing on the basketball team and walking me home from school and eating lunch with me and Liv and Emma and Sasha in the cafeteria?

"So, we came all this way together so that we won't be together," I said.

Once again, he remained silent.

"After today, will I ever see you again?" I asked.

"I'm not sure. It might be better if you never do see me again."

I stopped and spun him around so that he was facing me. "Is that what you want, to never see me again?"

"You know that isn't what I want, but I have no choice. I'm just an experiment."

"No, you're not! You're a human being with feelings and with rights."

"It's not the same for me."

"For somebody who's smart, you're one of the stupidest people I've ever met. Tell me, what percent of genetics do a chimpanzee and a person share?"

"We share ninety-eight point eight percent of our DNA."

"And how about the differences between any two people?" I asked.

"We all share at least ninety-nine point nine percent of the same genetics."

"So just how different do you think you are from me? Just because you think *faster* doesn't mean you think *differently*. They sent you out in the world to find out what would happen to you, and we're what happened, whether they saw it coming or not. You're more than an experiment now. You're my boyfriend."

"That's the thing I'm most proud of."

"You're smarter than anybody else, but you're still just a human, and humans get to make choices. *You* get to make choices."

"So do you," Gene said.

He put the briefcase down and started pulling things out of it. He looked at some of the images and put them back. Others remained in his hand. I could tell from the size, from the greater areas of gray, that those were my scans.

"I'm going to do something I should have done in the beginning. You're no longer going to be part of the experiment. I'm going to destroy your scans."

"But don't they have other copies?"

"These are the originals. They made sure the hospital copies were deleted for security reasons. It wasn't your choice to be part of the experiment, and now it should be your decision to no longer be part of it."

He handed me a book of matches and the scans. There was my brain, staring back at me.

"You once told me that you knew I loved you from looking at one of these scans."

"Yes, the subtle changes in brain activity and functioning were highly indicative of a reaction to emotional attachment," he said.

I laughed. "You are such a romantic."

I reached up, put my arms around his shoulders, pulled him down, and kissed him. It was long and warm and passionate. He held me tight, wrapped in his arms, and I never wanted it to end. Was this the last time I'd ever kiss him?

He looked deeply into my eyes.

"I love you," I said.

"Becky, I love you more than life, in a way that I never even knew was possible."

My whole body felt warm and mushy, and my head was practically buzzing.

"We don't have much time before the compound security team arrives. We triggered a laser trip wire about two minutes ago. You have to burn the scans now, before they arrive."

I struck a match and went to touch it against the scan. I could simply set them on fire and I'd be out of the experiment.

"What if I don't want to be out? What if I want to continue to be part of it?"

"You want to be part of the experiment?"

"I want to be part of whatever is you," I said.

I heard engines in the distance. It sounded like they were coming from the other side of the ridge directly in front of us.

"I can't guarantee what's going to happen next," he said.

"Life doesn't come with guarantees. Neither does love."

He put the scans back into the briefcase, and at the same instant an ATV leaped over the ridge, and then a second and a third and a fourth. Each had two men dressed all in black with their faces covered, and they were armed.

"No guarantees, but you have my promise: I'll take care of you."

"Funny, I thought I was the one who was supposed to take care of you," I said.

The vehicles skidded to a stop, and the men jumped off, running, their rifles aimed at us. Involuntarily, I went to raise my arms, but Gene reached out and took me by the hand instead, holding tightly.

We were surrounded.

The man at the very front removed his mask. He was smiling.

"Lower your weapons," he ordered, and everybody did as they were told. They also pulled down their masks. They all were smiling, and they all looked friendly.

The lead man walked over. "Gene, it's good to see you."

"It's good to see you, Captain."

Gene extended his hand. The man reached out, and they shook.

"And this must be Becky," he said.

I just nodded, too stunned and too relieved to say anything.

The captain reached up and pushed a button on a little radio attached to his collar. "We have secured the intruders. It's Gene, and he has Becky, and they're safe."

There was a roar of applause over the radio from the other end.

"We're bringing them in now."

"Roger that," came the reply.

"I don't know exactly how you managed to do this," the captain said. "But I think I've learned not to underestimate what you can do."

"Could you let Becky's parents know she's safe?" Gene asked.

"I could, or she could tell them herself. They're in the compound."

"My parents are here!" I gasped. I couldn't believe it.

"We brought them in to make sure they were safe."

"And they know what happened? What really happened?" I asked.

"As much as we could tell them. Now, let's go and see them."

Gene pulled me closer. "Becky, I don't know what's going to come next, but I know it's going to be all right."

"It's going to be all right because we're together."

"The way it was meant to be," he said. "After all, if you think about it, I really was made for you."

ERIC WALTERS began writing in 1993 as a way to entice his grade five students into becoming more interested in reading and writing. Walters has now published 120 novels and picture books. His novels have become bestsellers, have been translated into 16 languages, and have won over a hundred awards, including eight Forest of Reading awards and the 2020 Governor General's Literary Award. He conceived of the I Read Canadian Day and is a tireless presenter, speaking to over 100,000 students per year across North America. In 2014, Walters was named a Member of The Order of Canada. He lives in Guelph, Ontario, with his wife, Anita, and they have three grown children — Christina, Nicholas, and Julia — and six grandchildren.

We acknowledge the sacred land on which Cormorant Books operates. It has been a site of human activity for 15,000 years. This land is the territory of the Huron-Wendat and Petun First Nations, the Seneca, and most recently, the Mississaugas of the Credit River. The territory was the subject of the Dish With One Spoon Wampum Belt Covenant, an agreement between the Iroquois Confederacy and Confederacy of the Ojibway and allied nations to peaceably share and steward the resources around the Great Lakes. Today, the meeting place of Toronto is still home to many Indigenous people from across Turtle Island. We are grateful to have the opportunity to work in the community, on this territory.

We are also mindful of broken covenants and the need to strive to make right with all our relations.